Here's what critics are saying about the *Hollywood Headlines M*

"Gemma Halliday's witty, entertaining writir
through in her new book! I look forward to seeing
Tina as this series continues. A fun read!"
  - Fresh Fiction

MYSTERY

"(*HOLLYWOOD SCANDALS)* is a great start to a new
series that I will definitely be following as Halliday writes the
kind of books that just make you smile and put you in a great
mood. They're just so enjoyable and I would without a doubt
recommend this book to romance and mystery readers alike."
  - Enchanted By Books

"(*HOLLYWOOD SCANDALS)* is very well written with
smart and funny dialogue. It is a well-paced story that is
thoroughly enjoyable with a mystery, a little romance, and a lot
of laughs. Readers are sure to enjoy this delightful tale which is
highly recommended."
  - Romance Reviews Today

"The latest in the Hollywood Headlines series is 320 pages
of pure fun. Halliday has created yet another laugh-out-loud
whodunit. She breathes life into her mystery with a rich cast of
vivid, pulp-fiction type characters and a heroine worth rooting
for. 4 1/2 stars!"
  - RT Book Reviews

BOOKS BY GEMMA HALLIDAY

Hollywood Headlines Mysteries:
Hollywood Scandals
Hollywood Secrets
Hollywood Confessions

High Heels Mysteries:
Spying in High Heels
Killer in High Heels
Undercover in High Heels
Alibi in High Heels
Mayhem in High Heels
Christmas in High Heels (short story)
Sweetheart in High Heels (short story)

Other Works:
Viva Las Vegas
Haunted (novella)
Watching You (short story)
Confessions of a Bombshell Bandit (short story)

HOLLYWOOD CONFESSIONS

---

a Hollywood Headlines mystery

GEMMA HALLIDAY

For reality stars everywhere.
May there always be more roses to hand out, more tribal players to eliminate, more stars to dance with, and more idols to vote for.

Chapter One

"Well, we are all very impressed with your *body* of work, Miss Quick."

Was he talking about my tits?

I wasn't sure, but I nodded at the man sitting across from me anyway. Balding, paunchy, nondescript gray suit. Your typical managing editor.

"Thank you, Mr. Callahan," I said, keeping my voice as even as possible, despite the anxiety that had been building throughout our interview. He and I both knew my portfolio contained a very small body of work. So small that I almost hadn't even bothered submitting it when I'd heard the *L.A. Times* was looking to fill a desk. I'd only been a working reporter for just under a year, not long compared to most veteran newshounds. Then again, it was the *L.A. Times*. I'd have to be a moron not to at least apply for the job. And, moron was one thing I was not.

"I've shown your clippings to my colleagues, and they all agreed that your *assets* would be a wonderful addition to the paper." He glanced down at my chest.

Yeah, he was totally talking about my tits.

I shifted in my seat, adjusting my neckline. I knew I should have gone for a higher-cut blouse, but this one matched the pink pinstripes in my skirt so perfectly.

"Wonderful," I said, giving him a big offer-me-a-salary smile.

"After consulting with my assistant editor, we've decided we'd like to offer you a freelance opportunity here at the *L.A. Times*."

"Really?" I did a mental fist pump, and even though I was trying my best to play it cool, I heard my voice rise an octave, sounding instead of a professional business woman more like a kid who'd just been told she could have ice-cream for dinner. "Ohmigod, that would be…wow. Really?"

He nodded, a grin spreading across his paunchy cheeks. "Really. Now, I know you were hoping for a staff position, but if this opportunity goes well there's a chance to transition from freelance into something more permanent."

Freelance, staff, one-shot deal, I didn't care. It was the *L.A. Times*! The holy grail of any reporter's career. And they wanted me! I had died and gone to heaven.

"That sounds great! Amazing. Wow, thanks."

"Wonderful! We think you'll be perfect to write a weekly women's interest column."

I felt my face freeze mid goofy grin. "Women's interest…you mean, like, relationship stuff?"

"No, no," he said, shaking his head. "Nothing so limiting."

"Oh, good."

"Not just relationships. We'd love for you to write about *anything* important to women. Lipstick, shoes, cleaning product reviews."

I felt that ice-cream dinner melting into a soft, mushy puddle. "Cleaning product reviews?"

He nodded, his jowls wobbling with aftershocks. "And lipstick and shoes. You know, women's subjects."

I felt my eyes narrowing. "Mr. Callahan, I graduated at the top of my class from UCLA. Didn't you read my resume? I'm an *investigative journalist*. I write stories, hard-hitting news stories. Did you see the one I wrote about the misappropriation of campaign funds last fall?"

"I did."

"And the Catholic Church scandal?"

"Sure."

"And the way I busted that story about middle-school drug dealers in the heights wide open?"

He nodded again. "Yes, they were all very good," he said. "But?"

"Miss Quick, we are a serious paper here."

"And I'm a serious journalist!"

He looked down at my skirt, the tiny frown between his bushy eyebrows clearly not convinced that serious reporters wore pink.

"Mr. Callahan," I tried again, the desperation in my voice clear even to my ears, "I know I may not have the experience that many of your reporters do, but I'm a hard worker. I love long hours, overtime, and I will do anything to get the story."

"I'm sorry, Miss Quick. But my assistant and I have reviewed your file, and we both agree that someone with your…" he paused, "…*assets* would best serve us writing a women's column." His eyes flickered to my chest again then looked away so fast I could tell his mandatory corporate sensitivity training had been a success.

But not so fast that I didn't catch him.

I narrowed my eyes. "Thirty-four D."

Mr. Callahan blinked. "Excuse me?"

"The pair of tits you've been staring at for the last hour? They're a thirty-four D."

"I…I…" he stammered, his cheeks tingeing red.

"And if you like that number, I have a few more for you," I said, gaining steam. "One-thirty-four: my I.Q. Twenty-three-eighty-five: my SAT score. Four-point-O: my grade point average at UCLA. And finally," I said, standing and hiking my purse onto my shoulder, "Zero: the chance that I will degrade not only myself but my entire gender by writing a column that supposes having ovaries somehow limits our intelligence level to complexities of eyeshadow and sponge mops."

Mr. Callahan stared at me, blinking beneath his bushy brows, his mouth stuck open, jowls slack on his jaw.

But I didn't give him a chance to respond. Instead I forced one foot in front of the other as I marched back through the busy newsroom that I would not be a part of, down the hallways of my dream paper, and out into the deceptively optimistic sunshine.

I made it all the way to my VW Bug before I let my indignation and anger morph into big, fat tears. Goddammit, I was not just a pair of headlights and a short skirt! I had a brain, a pretty damned functional one, if I did say so myself. I was a smart, diligent reporter.

But all anyone at any of the major newspapers I'd interviewed with since graduation had seen was Allie Quick: 36, 26, 36.

Seriously, you'd think boobs wouldn't be such a novelty in L.A.

I wiped my cheeks with the back of my hand, slid into my car and slammed my door shut, taking out my aggression on Daisy (Yes, I named my car. But don't worry, I'd stopped just short of putting big daisy decals on the side doors. I only had one small daisy decal on the trunk. A pink one. To match the pink silk Gerbera daisy stuck in my dash.). I immediately slipped my polyester skirt off and threw it in the backseat. Hey, it was California. It was summer. And my air conditioning had broken three paychecks ago. Don't worry, I had a pair of bikini bottoms on underneath. Then I pulled out of the parking lot and pointed my car toward the 101 Freeway.

My life hadn't always been like this. I'd grown up in a normal, suburban home in Reseda. I'd never known my dad, but Mom did a pretty decent job of keeping me in grilled cheese sandwiches and the latest trends in sneakers while building up her own wedding planning business. In fact, she'd built it so well that by the time I hit college, we were living pretty nicely. Unfortunately, Mom had died unexpectedly my junior year. So unexpectedly, she hadn't left a will. Everything had gone into probate, and once all her business creditors were paid, along with probate fees and the attorney I'd hired to get her stuff out of probate, there was *just* enough left for me to finish journalism school. But not much more. Which had been fine. I'd never expected to live off Mom forever, but I also hadn't expected how hard it would be for the valedictorian of her class to land a job at a newspaper.

At least, one that didn't involve cleaning product reviews.

I exited the freeway, traveling through the Hollywood streets until I pulled up to a squat, stuccoed building on Hollywood Boulevard stuck between two souvenir shops. At one time the building might have been white, but years of smog and rainless winters had turned it a dingy grey. The windows were covered in cheap vertical blinds, and a distinct odor of stale take-out emanated from the place.

I looked up at the slightly askew sign above the door. The *L.A. Informer*, my current place of employment. A tabloid. The lowest form of journalism in the known universe. I felt familiar shame curl in my belly at the fact that I actually worked here.

At last it was a step above sponge mops.

Maybe.

A very small one.

I pulled Daisy into a space near the back of the lot with a

sigh, slipping my skirt back over my hips before trudging up the one flight of stairs to the offices.

The interior was buzzing as usual, dozens of reporters hammering out the latest celebrity gossip on their keyboards to the tune of ringing telephones and beeping IMs. My cube was in the center of the room, just outside the door of my editor's glass-walled office. Luckily, at the moment his back was turned to me, a hand to his Bluetooth, shouting at someone on the other side just loudly enough that I could hear the occasional muffled expletive.

I ducked my head down, slipping into my chair before he could notice what a long lunch I'd taken. I quickly pulled up the story I'd been working on before I left that morning: Megan Fox's boobs—real, or fake.

Yeah, CNN we were not.

Swallowing down every dream I'd ever had of following in Diane Sawyer's footsteps, I hammered out a 2- by 3-inch column on the size, shape and possible plasticity of the actress's chest. I was just about finished (concluding that, duh, there was no way those puppies were organic), when an IM popped up on my screen. My editor.

Where have you been?

I peeked up over the top of my cube. He was still shouting into his earpiece but was now seated at his computer, eyes on the 32-inch flat screen mounted on his desk.

I ducked back down. *At lunch.*

Pretty long lunch.

I bit my lip. I was hungry.

There was a pause. Then: *Come into my office in three minutes.*

Great. Busted.

I glanced at the time on my computer. 1:42. I finished up my article, hit save, and two minutes and forty-three seconds later got up from my chair, smoothed my skirt, puckered to redistribute my lipgloss and pushed through the glass doors of his office to face the music.

He was still on the phone, nodding at what the guy on the other end said. "Yes. Fine. Great," came his lilting British accent. He motioned for me to sit in one of the two folding chairs in front of his desk. I did, tugging at my hem again as I watched him pace the office.

Felix Dunn was somewhere between late thirties and early forties, at least a good ten years my senior. Old enough that fine laugh lines creased the corners of his mouth, but young enough that his sandy blonde hair was cut in the same shaggy style I'd seen high school skateboarders wear. He was tall with the lean lines of a runner, though I'd never actually seen him jog. He was dressed today in his usual uniform of a pair of khaki pants and a white button-down shirt, paired with tan Sketchers. His clothes were wrinkled, looking like he'd slept in them, and his hair stood up just a little on top. I would've said he was pulling a casual chic thing, but I knew Felix well enough to know it was more laziness than a practiced look.

Not that Felix couldn't afford to look every bit the metrosexual , but he had his own priorities. He was what you'd call a cheap rich guy. He lived in a multi-million dollar home in the Hollywood Hills, thanks to old family money, but still opted to buy his socks on sale at the drugstore. I'd heard a rumor going around the office that he was actually a British lord, some distant relation to the queen, but he always seemed to have left his wallet at home when the check came at lunch.

"Listen, I've got a meeting now," Felix said into his earpiece. "I've got to go, but I'll call you tomorrow." He hit the end button on his Bluetooth then turned to me without skipping a beat. "The Megan Fox bit, where are we?"

"Done. Just need to proof it, and it'll be on your desk."

"Conclusion?"

"They're fake."

"You're sure?"

I gave him a look. "Seriously? I had more faith in your boob connoisseur status."

He shook his head as if disappointed. "Can't trust anything to be authentic these days."

"If it makes you feel any better, her ass is real."

He grinned. "I'm ecstatic. Listen, I have a new story I want you to work on."

Even though I knew it likely involved the man vs. natural-made status of a celebrity's body parts, I still got a little surge of adrenalin in my belly. I couldn't help it. I loved the thrill of ferreting out the truth, making sense of a chaotic series of facts. I hadn't been lying when I told Mr. Callahan at the *Times* that I lived for the story.

"Shoot," I told Felix. "I'm all ears."

"It involves—"

But he didn't get to finish. The door to his office flew open again and one of the other reporters, burst through. She had violet hair and wore a hot-pink baby-T featuring a picture of Oscar the Grouch and black jeans with little skulls on the back pockets over a pair of shit-kicker black boots. Tina Bender.

"I got it!" she said triumphantly, holding a photo high above her head.

Felix raised an eyebrow her way. "And what might 'it' be?"

"The frickin' story of the century." She slammed the photo down on Felix's desk.

He leaned forward to get a good look. I did the same.

The photo was of the outside of a gated home. If I had to guess, I'd say a mansion somewhere nearby. Beverly Hills or Malibu, if the palms lining the impressive driveway were any indication.

"Chester Barker's estate," Tina said, confirming my suspicions. "In Beverly Hills."

Felix leaned in. "The dead producer?"

Tina nodded. "Murdered, to be precise. This was taken just before his body was found by the maid."

I remembered the story. Chester Barker, a reality TV show producer, was found dead in his Beverly Hills estate two weeks ago, face-down on his bathroom floor and foaming at the mouth. At first the consensus had been accidental drug overdose, but upon further inspection the police had found evidence that Barker had been drugged on purpose. The verdict of murder had sent the media—both tabloid and legit—into a virtual feeding frenzy, the *Informer* staff included. Personally, I'd been searching high and low for any angle on Barker for days.

Unfortunately it appeared Tina had found it first.

"Where did you get this photo?" Felix asked.

"One of my informants."

Tina had informants all over Hollywood, her network

farther reaching than Verizon's. Something I sorely envied. The first thing they'd taught us in journalism class was that a reporter was only as good as her informants. And unfortunately, Tina's outnumbered mine ten to one.

"Check out the right corner," she said, pointing to the picture.

Felix and I did, both leaning in. In the corner of the picture, near the iron gates, was a figure, his back to the camera, a baseball cap with a squiggly red snake on the brim of it pulled low on his head.

"Who's that?" I asked.

Tina ignored me. As always. For some reason, she and I had gotten off on the wrong foot when I'd first come on board here. Probably because Felix had given me her biggest story right off the bat. While I'd felt kinda bad for her, my bank account had been hovering low enough that my Visa was rejected at the dollar store. I needed the job, and I'd needed that story to prove to Felix I deserved a paycheck, despite my minuscule portfolio. So, despite feeling sorry for Tina's loss, I'd taken the story and run with it. Luckily I'd delivered, Felix had kept me on, and my bank account now afforded me the luxury of shopping at Walmart's clearance bin.

I know, decadent.

But Tina had never forgiven me, and a hard and fast rivalry between the two of us had been born.

"Who's that?" Felix asked, repeating my query.

Predictably, Tina did *not* ignore him. "That, my dear editor, is Chester Barker's killer."

Felix raised an eyebrow.

She shrugged. "Or at least, it could be. A shadowy figure seen outside the mansion at the time of the death. Pretty suspicious, huh?"

Felix nodded, eyes still on the photo. "Any idea who our suspicious character is?"

She shook her head. "But I am *so* on this story. Give me twenty-four hours, and I'll have his name, address and credit score."

Felix bit the inside of his cheek for a moment, thinking over the proposition. Finally he said, "Okay. Run with it. The Barker story is all yours, Tina."

Her grin was twice the size of her face. "Ay-ay, chief!" She gave him a mock salute before fairly skipping out the door.

Felix pulled out a magnifying glass, training it on the photo. I waited while he silently scrutinized the shadowy figure, trying to make out any identifying marks.

Finally I couldn't take it anymore. I cleared my throat.

Felix's eyes jolted upward, as if surprised to still find me there.

"Uh, you said you had a story for *me*?"

"Oh. Right. Allie. Yeah." He cleared his throat, setting the photo of the would-be killer aside. "I got a tip this morning that Pippi Mississippi changed her hair color. I want you to go talk to her hairdresser and either confirm or deny."

Tina got a murder, and I got a dye job. Figures. Even at a tabloid no one took my journalism skills seriously.

Chapter Two

Jennifer Wood was the young teen actress who played the title character Pippi Mississippi on the hit tween cable show, launching not only the teen's acting career but also a singing contract, a line of clothing for eight-year-olds and a fragrance called "Totally Pippi" sold at finer department stores everywhere. Last year Jennifer starred in her big screen debut, *Pippi Mississippi: The Movie*, which had opened to the highest box office take since James Cameron's latest, launching Pippi into the realm of mega-celebrities. I think it was safe to say that Pippi Watching had officially passed baseball as America's favorite pastime.

Sadly, a picture of Pippi's new 'do in the *Informer* would probably outsell copies of *Time* with the president's picture on it.

According to the Hollywood grapevine, Pippi got her hair done at Fernando's salon, a Beverly Hills staple nestled smack in the center of the BH golden triangle, where real estate was worth an arm and a leg, and noses were changed as often as the seasons.

I pushed through the glass front doors of Fernando's, immediately assaulted by the scents of hair dye, frying perms and botanical conditioners with French names. The interior of the salon was done in a minimalist chic style—plain white walls, white sofa in the waiting area, white marble tiles on the floor and white plastic chairs at every station lining the middle of the salon floor. Two large red paintings were an unexpected splash of color along the back wall, providing one bold focal point.

The guy behind the reception desk provided the other. "Allie, love of my life, how are you, dahling!" he shouted, coming at me with air-kisses.

"Great, Marco." I air-smooched him back and gave a little shoulders-only hug.

Marco was a slim, Hispanic guy with eyeliner thicker than Tammy Faye's, outfits louder than Lady Gaga's and a vocabulary straight out of the movie *Clueless*. He was currently holding a bottle of sparkly silver glitter in one hand and a glue stick in the other. I almost hesitated to ask. "What's with the glitter?"

Marco looked down at the bottle in his hand. "We're having a sale on conditioner. I'm sprucing up the sign a little."

I looked over at his desk. A generic "sale" sign now had a glittery silver "20%" drawn across it in scrolling script.

"Very…sparkly."

"Thank you!" Marco beamed like a proud papa. "So, what can I do for you, dahling? We're on a tight schedule today, but for you I could bump someone."

"I appreciate the sentiment, Marco, but I'm actually here for…" I leaned in and whispered, "a little information."

He closed his heavily lined eyes and shook his head in the negative. "Sorry, dahling, no can do. You know my lips are sealed. What would happen if I tongue-wagged about every celebutant who came through here? I'd be out on my hot little fanny, that's what."

I grinned. "You know that would never happen. Fernando couldn't function without you."

Marco pursed his lips. Then nodded. "Well, that's true."

"Listen, I just need a confirm or deny over a new hair color."

He shook his head again. "Sorry. I have taken the celebrity hairdresser's oath. 'What happens in the salon stays in the salon.'"

"Hmmm." I narrowed my eyes. "What if I made it worth your while?"

He raised one drawn-in eyebrow at me. "Worth my while?"

"I happen to have an informant that happens to follow the club scene very closely. And happens to know where one very desirable celebrity is planning on partying this very evening."

Marco leaned in. "I'm intrigued. A-lister?"

I shrugged. "At least a B-plus."

"Who?"

I looked over both shoulders, trying to match his level of drama as I leaned in and whispered, "Adam Lambert."

"Shut the front door!" Marco said, almost spilling his glitter on the marble floor. "Where?"

"I'll tell you…if you can tell me a little something."

He narrowed his eyes at me. "Ooh, you are wicked, girl.

Fine. You cracked me." He paused, looked over both shoulders for prying ears then nodded, setting finger to the side of his nose. "Come into my office, dahling."

He turned and led the way through the salon. I followed him past buzzing drying stations and flying straight razors until we hit a door at the back. He opened it, doing an exaggerated over the shoulder again, and led the way inside.

I followed, trying not to smirk as I saw we were in a supply closet. Very cloak-and-dagger.

"So, what do you want to know?" he asked in a low whisper.

"Jennifer Wood. Is it true Pippi Mississippi has a new hair color?"

"Ah." He steepled his fingers. "She was in here the other day."

"And?"

"And America's favorite blonde teeny bopper?"

"Yes?"

"Now a redhead."

Bingo. "I don't suppose you got any pictures of her?"

He looked offended. "I don't suppose I did! What do you think I am, some sort of gossip?" Heaven forbid. "But," he said.

"But?"

"*Fernando* did take a snapshot for his wall of fame."

Double bingo.

"I'll throw in Adam's home address if you get me a copy."

Marco squealed like a second grader. "Done!" Then he scuttled off to find the picture in question.

I exited his "office" and sat down in the all white lobby to wait. While I did, I browsed through Fernando's magazine selection. Three out of four had Chester Barker's picture plastered on the front.

God, I wanted that story.

And not just because Tina had it, though I'll admit, after the way she'd gloated this afternoon, the thought of besting her did give me warm fuzzies. But Barker's death was the kind of serious story that serious journalists covered. *L.A. Times* serious, even. If I had that kind of story under my belt maybe I wouldn't be automatically relegated to the fluff pages.

I grabbed the magazine on top, this week's *People*, and began flipping through their take on Barker's death, complete with lots of glossy photos. I was about a page and a half in when the glass front doors beside me opened, and a tall woman walked in. She was dressed in black, form-fitting yoga pants and a tight little T-shirt. Her blonde hair was pulled back in ponytail, and she wore a ball cap pulled down low over her face.

I froze, staring at her cap. It was black with a red squiggly snake on the brim. Just like the mystery man in Tina's photos.

No. Way.

I blinked back surprise as I watched her cross the salon and greet one of the stylists, who quickly ushered her into a room in the back. I jumped up from the sofa to follow her, just as Marco re-emerged from the back with a framed photo of Pippi Mississippi in hand.

"Okay, here's your pic-ey! Just do not under any circumstance reveal where you got it, because if Fernando found out—"

I grabbed him by the shoulders mid-sentence. "The woman who just came in here. In the ballcap. Do you know who she is?"

"Ay, easy on the shirt, chica. It's an Armani."

My grasp tightened. "The woman, Marco. It's important."

"Okay, okay. Geeze, girl. It's Dana Dashel."

I gave him a blank look. "Who?"

"You know, from that HBO series *Lady Justice*? She plays the porn lawyer."

"Riiiiiight…" I knew the show. It was this season's naughty breakout hit about a mild-mannered woman who inadvertently becomes the go-to-attorney for porn stars. Lots of stars, lots of scandal, very little clothing. A no-brainer to top the ratings.

"Listen, I have to talk to her," I told Marco, still grasping his shoulders.

He shook his head. "No can do, honey. She's an exclusive client. Photos are one thing, but I cannot have a tabloid reporter conducting interviews in here. Unless you're her bikini waxer, there is no way you are getting into that room."

I looked from Marco to the closed door, desperation bubbling up in my throat. But I could tell by the look on his face that this time he really wasn't cracking. "Fine," I said. "Look, email me a copy of Pippi's photo and I'll send back the deets on Adam's party tonight, cool?"

Marco looked immeasurably relived. "That I can do."

"Thanks," I said then turned to go. I slipped out the glass doors, watching over my shoulder as Marco took the photo out of its frame and to his desk, fussed a little with his scanner, and popped the photo back into its frame. A minute later he picked it up and headed back to the back of the salon to re-hang it.

The second his back was turned I pushed through the front doors again and half-walked, half-jogged past the cut and color stations to the storeroom Marco had used as his "office". Once inside I grabbed a white coat from the shelf. I thrust it on then peeked out of the door. Marco was back at the reception desk, his back to me. I quickly slipped out of the storeroom and crossed the three big steps to the waxing room Dana occupied. I opened the door and went inside, shutting it behind me with a soft click.

The blonde lay on a table in the center of the sterile room, a white sheet covering her body. Her eyes were closed, a tiny lavender scented pillow draped across them. On a chair beside her sat her yoga clothes, and on top of them the ball cap. No doubt about it, it was the same one the shadowy figure outside Barker's had worn.

Maybe my luck was turning.

Standing over Dana was a woman wearing a coat identical to mine and an expression that said she clearly had not expected to be interrupted.

"May I help you?" she asked, though the tone in her voice was more, *What the hell are you doing in my waxing room?*

"Uh…yes," I said, clearing my throat. "I'm …here to wax Dana."

She raised an eyebrow my way. "*You* are?"

"Fernando asked that I take this one. As a personal favor."

"And you are?"

"Allie. I'm new here."

She frowned, biting the corner of her lip. "Okay. I guess," she said. Then handed me a tub of gooey stuff that smelled like more lavender. "She's all yours," she said, walking out.

I looked down at the prone actress, lying perfectly still on the table. I wondered if she was asleep or just going into a zen-like state in anticipation of the wax to come.

I looked down at the tub in my hands, stirring the wooden stick. Not to get into TMI territory, but I've never been a huge fan of waxing. Mostly because I'm not a huge fan of pain. Just once I'd been suckered into it. I'd been up late watching infomercials, and some Australian woman came on touting a no-pain waxing kit. I'd ordered one (Hey, they weren't sold in stores, and they threw in a second kit absolutely free!), and as soon as it arrived in the mail (just four to six weeks later) I'd smothered my legs in the patented wax formula, applied the reusable organic cotton strips and let 'er rip.

I howled louder than my neighbor's cat in heat. No pain, my ass! My legs had been covered in red stripes for a week. I'd been a strictly Nair gal ever since.

"I have to be on set in an hour," the woman beneath the sheet said, jarring me from my painful memory. "So, not to rush you, but..." she trailed off.

"Right. Sure."

I looked down at the items the white-coated woman had set out on the side table. A pile of little white, cotton strips and a bottle of essential oils. Okay, sure. Easy. What was there to it but wax on, wax off, right?

I stirred the lavender-scented goop again as I lifted the sheet to reveal my starlet au natural.

I scooped a bit of the wax with my wooden stick then slapped it on her inner thigh. "So," I said, smoothing out the warm glob. "You are awesome on *Lady Justice*."

"Thanks," Danae said, eyes still closed behind her relaxation pillow. "It's a great show to work on. The writers are awesome."

"Yeah. I can tell." I laid a white cotton strip down on the wax glob. I gritted my teeth and pulled.

Dana jumped. "Holy hell!"

I winced. "Sorry." Though I noticed fine hairs on the strip I'd pulled away. Okay, so far so good.

I laid down another glob of wax next to the bare spot, moving inward. "I guess you must meet a lot of interesting people on the show?"

"Sure," she agreed. "A lot of porn stars come guest for us. Though I wish they didn't show quite so much skin. Makes it hard for people to take me seriously as an actress—holy mother of God!" Dana jumped on the table as I ripped another strip off.

"Sorry," I mumbled again, watching her skin redden. On the up side, it was smooth as a baby's butt.

"That's okay," she gritted through her teeth. "No pain, no bikini, right?"

"Right." I laid down another glob just that much farther inward.

"So, speaking of interesting people…did Chester Barker work on your show?"

"Barker?"

"Yeah. The producer?"

"Oh, right. The dead guy." She paused a moment. "Not that I know of. Why?"

"Oh, no reason. I just wondered if you knew him. Or had ever visited his house," I said, watching her expression closely. (Well, as closely as I could with half her face obscured under the scented pillow.)

She shrugged under the sheet. "I think I might have met him once at a party or something. But, no, I've never seen his house." She paused. "Why do you want to know about his place?"

Actually, I could care less about his place. It was who had been there the night of his murder I was interested in. "Oh, no reason," I lied. "I just heard it was a spectacular mansion, that's all."

"Oh. Well, I wouldn't know."

Bummer. I mentally recalculated my tactic as I laid down another cotton strip and pulled.

"Hot damn!" Dana's right foot jumped in the air, narrowly avoiding the tub of wax in my hands. "You sure you know what you're doing? Olga's waxes never hurt quite this much."

"Sorry," I said on autopilot. "Hey, you know, that was a great hat you were wearing when you came in," I said, gesturing the ballcap on the chair.

"What? Oh, right. Yeah, thanks."

"It looks very unique. I've never seen that design before." I laid another glob of wax down, this one ensuring she could go

Brazilian.

"Actually," Dana responded, "they handed those hats out to everyone on the *Lady Justice* set at the beginning of the season."

"Oh." I felt my spirits sink, my chance at hopping on the Barker train slipping through my fingers. "Everyone got one?"

She nodded. "Yep. Everyone on set that day. All the cast, crew, producers, everyone."

Great. That was what, like, two hundred people? So much for narrowing my suspect down.

"Oh, hey! You know what?"

"What?" I asked, laying down the next cotton strip.

"You were asking about Barker's place earlier, right?"

"Yes?"

"Well, one of the execs who works on our show might know more about what his home was like. He's Barker's business partner. Or was, I guess."

Lucky streak, here I come. "Barker's partner worked on *Lady Justice*?" I confirmed.

"Yep. He was on set all season."

"So, he would own one of these ballcaps too?"

"Um, I guess so."

"What's his name?"

"Alec Davies."

What did you want to bet that the shadowy figure outside Barker's was Alec Davies? "Fabulous. Thanks!" I said.

Then I ripped the last white strip off.

In hindsight, maybe my excitement at having a real lead made me a little too vigorous. Maybe I should have gone little more slowly. Maybe a little more gently. Maybe I should have waited for Olga.

"Sonofa—" Dana lifted off the table, her right foot kicking in the air, connecting squarely with the tub of wax in my hand. Which tipped over, spilling white, sticky stuff all over the floor.

And all over me.

I looked down. My pink blouse and pinstriped skirt were completely covered in wax, not to mention my hands, legs, and cleavage.

Dana pulled the lavender pillow off her eyes. "Oh, wow. Sorry." She frowned. "Maybe next time I should just ask for

Olga."

Ya think?

"I'll go get her now," I promised, feeling the wax set up as I slipped out the door.

I looked down at my watch. Twenty minutes until the *Informer* edition closed for the day. If I sped, there was a slim chance I could make it to the office before we went to print.

I ripped off the white coat (taking a few waxed arm hairs with it) and took my sticky self back out through the lobby.

"Allie?" Marco looked up, a wrinkle of confusion on his forehead. "What are you doing here again?"

Oops. I'd forgotten about him.

"Uh. Hi. I, uh, forgot something in the back..." I said, trailing off. I ducked my head down to cover my terribly delivered lie and made for the front doors.

Unfortunately, with my head ducked in shame, I failed to see the edge off Marco's desk, bumping into it. Which jostled the sign he'd been making. And the bottle of glitter. Dumping the entire thing down the front of me.

Glitter stuck to the semi-hardened wax, turning me into a kindergartener's project.

"Oh, honey," Marco said, a smirk playing at the corner of his mouth. "Look at you sparkle, girl!"

I closed my eyes, thought a really bad word then plowed my sparkly self out through the doors.

I looked down at my watch—4:42. I had 18 minutes left. I ran to my Bug, revved the engine and pulled into traffic down Wilshire while I simultaneously flipped my laptop open on the passenger seat beside me and powered it on. At the next red light, I opened my speech-to-type program. "A shadowy figure was seen outside Chester Barker's estate the night of his death, and we have an exclusive on his identity," I said out loud, watching the words appear as type on my screen.

The light changed, and I surged forward, continuing to dictate what I'd learned at Fernando's as I crossed town.

Exactly sixteen minutes later, I screeched into the lot of the *Informer,* grabbed my laptop and flew out of my car, not even bothering to beep it locked behind me.

I shoved through the building's front doors, stabbing the up button on the elevator. I waited a two count. Too long! I took the stairs two at a time in my heels, hit the second floor and ran into the newsroom, weaving through the cubes toward Felix's office. 4:59. Thirty seconds left. I didn't bother knocking, shoving my shoulder into Felix's door and pushing my way in.

Felix was behind his desk, Tina hovering just to his right, a piece of paper in hand. No doubt, her take on Barker's shadowy figure. I mentally crossed my fingers, hoping for once my informers trumped hers.

"Stop the presses!" I yelled. Cliché, I know. But I'd always wanted to say that. I dropped my computer down on Felix's desk with a thud.

He looked down at my laptop. Then up at me as I panted like an Olympic sprinter (The Stairmaster at the gym was one thing, but have you ever tried to run up metal fire stairs in three-inch heels and a miniskirt? I think I deserved at least the silver for that.).

Felix raised an eyebrow at the wax and glitter covering my entire person (and, incidentally, now all of my car upholstery), but had the good sense not to mention it. Instead, he gestured to my laptop and asked, "What's this?"

"The Chester Barker story you're running in tomorrow's edition."

He raised the other eyebrow but reserved comment, looking down at the copy typed on the screen.

Tina, on the other hand, never reserved her comments. "What the hell! Barker is *my* story, New Girl."

I hated it when she called me New Girl. I'd been here almost a year. And just because I was new didn't mean I wasn't good. New was fresh. New was hungry. And, I thought, not able to hide my smirk, new had just beaten her to the headline.

"Then I'm sure you know who the figure outside Chester's house is," I countered.

She opened her mouth to respond, did a couple guppy faces, and shut it. Clearly she did not.

"I take it you do?" Felix asked me, his eyes quickly scanning the copy.

I nodded triumphantly. "I do, indeed. Alec Davies."

Felix glanced up at me. "The producer?"

"Correct. And he was Chester Barker's partner."

"How did you get this information?" Tina asked, dancing around Felix, trying to read my copy over his shoulder.

I shrugged. "I have my sources."

"What kind of sources?" Felix pressed. "This is a pretty big accusation to make blind."

"The hat," I said. "The one with the snake on it that the figure was wearing in the photo? They gave them out to the cast and crew of *Lady Justice*. Davies worked on that show. He owns the hat."

"So must dozens of other people," Tina jumped in. "If they gave them to everyone on the set, it's hardly a one-of-a-kind."

"True," I conceded. "But, it's quite a coincidence. What are the chances anyone else on the set had that close of a connection to Barker?"

Felix paused a moment, taking in both of our arguments. Finally he said, "Well done, Allie."

I felt my chest swell with pride. "So you'll print it?"

Felix nodded slowly. "Let me read it over first, but if it's solid, yes, it'll lead tomorrow's edition."

Tina threw her hands up on the air. "Oh, come on! You gave *me* this story."

"Did you know about Davies?" Felix asked, turning on her.

"Well, no, not exactly. But I have some very good feelers out there right now."

"Great. Let me know when those pan out. In the meantime, Allie, I want you to follow up with Davies tomorrow at the studio. Find out what he was doing there and what he knows about Barker's death."

"Yes, sir!" I did a mock salute, glitter raining down onto his brown carpet.

Tina rolled her eyes. "I can't believe this shit. You're giving my headline to the glitter queen."

"Tina," Felix warned.

But she plowed ahead. "Though, why should I be surprised? It's no secret she's editor's pet."

"*Tina…*"

"I mean, we all know the only reason you even hired her was because she waltzed in here with her shirt unbuttoned to her navel and her skirt hiked to her doo-dah."

"Bender!" Felix shouted. "That's enough."

Tina shut her mouth with a click.

"If and when your leads get back to you, type it up," Felix barked. "Until then, Allie is lead on Barker. Do I make myself clear?"

Tina shot me a look that could freeze Mt. Saint Helens. "Crystal," she spit out.

"Good. Dismissed, Bender."

Tina turned and stalked out of the office, clomping her boots all the way back to her cube. I watched her go, feeling my satisfaction at besting her slowly slip down a notch. Felix never raised his voice. In fact, I'd only heard him do it once in all the time I'd known him. He was forceful, yes. Commanding, yes. But in true Brit fashion, he always kept a tight reign on his emotions.

So the fact that Tina had rattled him meant she must have hit a nerve.

I paused in the doorway. I knew I should just take my story and go. But instead of turning to go, that hit nerve had me turning back to my boss.

"Um, Felix?"

"What?" he asked. His eyes were still dark, flashes of navy shooting through them as his chest rose and fell faster than normal.

I bit my lip. "I have to ask…you gave me the story because I'm a good journalist, right?"

He gave me a blank look.

"What I mean is…what Tina said has no merit, right? When you hired me, it was totally because you knew what a great writer I was and that I would deliver copy and sell papers for you. And not…" I trailed off, feeling my cheeks burn, wishing I'd just left it alone.

Felix's eyes met mine, his sandy eyebrows still hovering menacingly over his blue eyes. "And not what, Allie? Spit it out."

I took a deep breath. And spit. "And not because we slept together?"

Chapter Three

My history with Felix was complicated, at best. Completely fucked up, at worst.

I'd first met Felix two years ago when he was the *Informer*'s top reporter and I was still studying journalism at UCLA. He'd been covering a story at the time, and I'd been fascinated at his information-gathering tactics, none of which they taught in my classes. Hacking databases, picking locks, breaking and entering. I was intrigued. Throw in the fact that Felix was not entirely hard on the eyes, and I'm woman enough to admit I'd had a teeny tiny schoolgirl crush on him.

Unfortunately, he'd also had a crush of his own at the time, and not on me. There was this fashion designer who was also involved in the story he was working on. And she was everything I was not—sophisticated, worldly and stylish enough to have walked out from a magazine cover. It wasn't hard to see how a college kid suddenly became invisible in her shadow.

Still, when Felix had let me tag along on his story, I'd jumped at the chance. In fact, I'd jumped so much that I ended up getting myself kidnapped by a killer, bound, gagged, and shoved in the back of a bakery van. I'd spent a day and a half surrounded by stale muffins and pure fear before Felix had tracked the killer down and come to my rescue.

That was when things had really become complicated between us. The fashion designer Felix was into? Well, as soon as the story wrapped up, she ran off to Vegas and married another guy. Felix was crushed and, lucky me, I was the closest blonde at hand when he went on the rebound.

The blonde he'd just swooped in and rescued action-hero style, causing my little crush to swell to ridiculous proportions. Ridiculous enough that I'd gone home with him, let one thing lead right into another, and I'd ended the evening between Felix's 500-thread-count Egyptian cotton sheets. Naked. On top of Felix.

Of course, in the morning we'd both realized with startling clarity what a mistake it had been. Felix was clearly still in love with the fashion designer, and I had acted like the pathetic equivalent of a journalism groupie.

So, we'd parted ways.

Or, more accurately, I'd dressed in the dark, claimed an early class and slunk out with my tail (and inside-out panties) between my legs.

It wasn't until a year later, after I'd graduated and was desperate for a job, that I'd contacted Felix again. He'd been promoted to managing editor by then and was the only person I knew working at an actual paper, even if it was a tabloid. I'd pleaded my case, telling him he was the only thing standing between me and certain starvation. Despite my lack of experience, he'd finally relented. Probably out of guilt. Possibly out of lust. For sure out of pity.

No matter the reason, I'd gratefully taken the job, and we'd maintained a professional editor/reporter relationship ever since, never once speaking of The Night.

Until now.

And, I could tell by the look on his face, he wished as much as I did that we'd maintained that silence.

"What?" he asked blinking at me.

"You heard me," I said, sticking to my guns even as a thick film of awkwardness settled over the room. "Did you hire me because I can write, or because we slept together?"

He didn't answer me right away. Instead his eyes narrowed, assessing me. So intently that I began to fidget, picking at the waxy glitter under my fingernails. Then finally he moved from the barrier behind the desk, crossed the room until he was standing in front of me. Close in front of me. So close I could smell warm coffee on his breath.

I licked my lips, fighting off the instinct to take one giant step back. The awkwardness in the air had shifted to something else. Just as thick. Just as potent. Ten times more uncomfortable.

Felix leaned in, coming almost nose to nose with me. His voice was low, intimate, barely audible above the humming newsroom just outside his door. "You might be good in bed, Allie, but if all you were was a great lay, I'd have fired you months ago."

I'm not sure what I expected him to say, but his frank language took me by surprise. I swallowed, opened my mouth to respond.

But he cut me off, stepping away and diffusing the moment as quickly as he'd charged it. "Go home. Quick. And tomorrow I want an interview with Davies on my desk by five. Sharp."

I cleared my throat and nodded. "Right. Five."

"And this lead better pan out," he warned me, "or the story is Tina's, no matter how low your necklines go."

I opened my mouth to protest, but it died on my tongue as I saw the corner of his lips quirk up. He was mocking me. Jerk.

"You'll have your story by *four*," I countered. Then pushed out of his office.

* * *

As much as I was itching to get to Davies, I knew Felix was right. The best time to catch him would be at the studios tomorrow. And it would probably be a good idea to conduct the interview sans glitter. So instead of diving into my headline story, I hopped in my Bug and headed toward home for a much-needed shower.

I lived in a one bedroom on the bottom level of a

fourplex on the outskirts of Glendale, tucked up against the foothills of the San Gabriel Mountains. It was as rural as you could get in L.A. Which didn't really mean *rural* rural, but trees lined the streets, the hills provided a backdrop of green when you could see them through the smog haze, and at night I only heard the distant hum of a single freeway instead of four. All in all, it was the most peaceful escape I could find on a tabloid reporter's budget.

I parked in my reserved spot beneath our building and took the stairs up to my place on the ground floor. While the outside of the building was standard Southern California grey stucco, I did my best to make the interior my own. The brown renter's carpet on the floor was covered in colorful throw rugs in shades of purple and pink. The free couch I'd gotten off Craigslist was covered in a white slipcover, accented by hot pink pillows I'd sewn myself, featuring little gold tassels at the corners. A vase of gerbera daisies sat on my pink coffee table, and I'd hand painted the plain wooden kitchen table and chairs with pink flowers and yellow smiley faces. My last boyfriend had said walking into my place was like walking into Barbie's dream apartment. I'll admit, it was a lot of pink. But pink made me happy. And if you can't be happy in your own home, what have you got?

I set my keys down on the pink end table by the door and grabbed the stack of mail that had been shoved through my door slot while I'd been at work. A Macy's bill, a Banana Republic bill, a Limited bill, and a coupon for half off graphic T's at Old Navy. I ripped the coupon out, put it in my purse then shoved the bills into the heart-shaped cookie jar on my counter. Seeing bills did not make me happy.

I took a quick shower, removing most of the glitter (though a couple patches of stubborn wax still clung to my ankles) then dug into the refrigerator for dinner. Half of a pizza and a salad with low-fat dressing stared back at me. I did a mental *eeenie meenie minie moe*, but it was pretty clear which one was going to win out. I opened the pizza box and indulged in a Hawaiian with extra pineapple. While it always made me feel better about myself to buy salad, it usually just sat in my fridge until it wilted, died, and I went out to buy more. I mentally calculated how much time I had to do on the stepper at the gym to make up for the Hawaiian calories and decided it was well worth it.

I took my pizza into the living room and plopped on the sofa. Immediately my lap was filled with a white, fluffy ball of purring fur.

"Well, hello, Mr. Fluffykins," I said. Yes, out loud. Call me crazy, but I talk to my cat. I fed him a piece of Canadian bacon as he pawed at my thighs, creating himself a nice little nest. I flipped on the TV and went to my DVR, scrolling through my recorded shows.

"Are we in the mood for Wolf Blitzer or Katie Couric?" I asked my cat.

Mr. Fluffykins cocked his head to the side and mewed.

"Couric it is." I selected the program and settled in to get my fill of what was going on in the news world that didn't revolve around a teenebrity's hair color.

* * *

I was jolted awake by a splash of water hitting my face and the sound of something slamming into the side of the building. My eyes shot open and I bolted upright in bed, adrenalin immediately pumping through my system. It was pitch-black. I blinked through the darkness, trying to get my bearings. Finally shapes came into focus...my Hello Kitty alarm clock, the flower-shaped mirror on my wall, Mr. Fluffykins dozing at my feet.

I was just about to write off my jolt as a bad dream when the sound erupted again. Water, hitting the side of my building with the velocity of a firehose. Instinctively I turned to the window... and felt water raining down on me.

I jumped up from my bed and watched as a stream of water shot through my window, landing on my pink bedsheets.

What the hell?

I pulled aside my plastic renter's blinds and peered out into the yard.

Between my building and the fourplex next door sat a strip of grass. At current there was more mud than greenery, but a few patch of crabgrass looked hopeful they might become a lawn one day.

Apparently so were my neighbors, as a brand-new, industrial-sized sprinkler head jutted out of the muddy crabgrass, spraying a rotating stream of water at dangerous speeds between the buildings. I jumped back when it turned my way again, narrowly avoiding another power blast as it shot through my window.

Unfortunately Mr. Fluffykins wasn't so lucky, getting the full force of it on his tail. He yowled and jumped almost as high I as had, running for the safety of the living room.

I quickly shut the window, making a mental note to visit my neighbors tomorrow morning. Then I looked down at my sheets.

Soaked.

Fab.

I grabbed a pillow and shuffled out after Mr. Fluffykins to the sofa.

Three hours and one fat, snoring cat later, I awoke with a crick in my neck, a pain in my side, and cat hair in my mouth.

Ick.

I looked at the clock. Six am.

I grabbed a cup of coffee then went into my room to survey the damage to my sheets in the light of day. It looked like I'd wet my bed. Several times. I stripped them off, trudged to the back of the building and threw them in the coin-operated laundry. I crossed the muddy lawn, now squishing wet beneath my fuzzy pink slippers, and banged on my neighbor's door.

Two beats later a squat, Russian guy answered. He had a bald head, a paunchy middle barely encased in a bathrobe, and a cigar sticking out the side of his face. "Dah?"

"I'm so sorry to bother you, but your sprinkler is turned up very too high."

He beamed. "Dah. Is good sprinkler, no?"

I shook my head. "No. Is not good. Is pelting my bedroom window."

His massive unibrow hunkered down over his beady eyes. "Too loud?"

"Too wet. The window was open, and it soaked my bed."

He grinned. "Ha! That wake you up, huh?"

I narrowed my eyes. "Oh, yeah. It wake me up."

He nodded. "Okay, okay. I fix it. Promise. Today, I fix it."

"Thanks," I mumbled, then trudged back home to take the longest, hottest shower on record. Seriously, if my paycheck didn't afford an apartment upgrade soon, I might shoot myself. Or my neighbor.

I went with peach-scented body wash today, needing the pick-me-up, then did my hair and make-up, adding an extra layer of mascara to show just how serious I was about this Barker story. I dressed in a white denim skirt, pink tank top with ruffles down the front and a pair of silver roman-style sandals with glittery glass diamonds on the top. Totally cute. Totally hot. Totally going to get me into any place I wanted to go, press pass or no.

Which was good, because Barker's production

company, Real Life Productions, was housed on the Sunset Studios lot. The Sunset Studios were located off the 101, just west of Griffith Park, in the heart of tinseltown. They were the largest studio in town, taking up two full city blocks, and surrounded by a large cement wall topped by massive spiky iron bars. San Quentin was easier to break into than the Sunset Studios. It was the only fortress in Hollywood impenetrable by the average reporter.

Luckily, I wasn't just average.

I grabbed a knock-off Juicy bag from my closet and matched it with a pair of big, black sunglasses. They looked just like Christian Dior shades, right down to the CD on the sides. I'd actually bought them at a gas station halfway between here and Oxnard, used a sharpie to obliterate the generic brand name, then glued on the sparkly "CD" with a hot glue gun. Not bad, even if I did say so myself.

Then, instead of jumping in my Bug, I dialed a car service and waited while it rang three times on the other end.

"Elite cars, how may I help you?" a woman answered the phone.

"Hi," I said, giving my voice just the slightest nasally tone to it. "This is Paris Hilton's assistant. I need a car to pick her up in Glendale at the Starbucks on Brand, and take her to the Sunset Studios in Hollywood."

"No problem," the woman on the other end said, and I could hear the sound of a keyboard keys as she typed info into her system. "When you would like it?" she asked.

"ASAP. She's shooting a commercial there this morning."

More typing. "Okay, we have a town car limousine that can pick her up in fifteen minutes. Will that be acceptable?"

"Fabulous!" I said.

"I just need a credit card to process the order, and I'll dispatch him right away."

"No problem," I said. Then rattled of the digits of the *Informer*'s account. Not that I was supposed to have unlimited access to such digits, but if Felix really hadn't wanted me using it, he shouldn't have left his card out where anyone could see it and memorize the number. Besides, this was a bona fide business expense. And not one I had the funds to cover, I realized, as the woman on the phone gave me the total.

I thanked her and hung up then wrapped a pink silk scarf over my head, put on my faux designer sunglasses, and hightailed it to Starbucks to wait for my limo.

It arrived exactly fifteen minutes later. The driver got out and opened the back door for me with a, "Good morning, Miss Hilton."

I gave him an aloof nod, hopped in and promptly closed the partition between us.

Twenty minutes later, the driver pulled up to the front gate of the Sunset Studios. I held my breath in the backseat, thinking heiress-like thoughts.

The driver stopped at the guardhouse and rolled down his window. A guy with a clipboard who didn't look a day over a hundred hobbled out of the tiny structure and up to the window. His skin was wrinkled and tanned to a crisp, like he'd spent one too many days on duty in the guardhouse without sunscreen. Or he really dug tanning beds.

I cracked the partition to hear the exchange.

"Name?" the guard asked.

"Elite car service. I've got Paris Hilton here."

The guard looked to my tinted window, squinting in. "Can you have her roll her window down, please?" he asked.

I felt butterflies take hold in my stomach as I slowly rolled down my window, praying the guard was a nearsighted as he seemed. I gave him a little wave.

The guard nodded. "'Morning, Miss Hilton," he said.

I did a sigh of relief.

"Go on ahead," the ancient guy said, waving the driver on and stepping back into his house.

That was almost too easy.

I quickly rolled up my window, instructing the driver to let me out near the production offices to the left.

Sunset Studios was a huge place, laid out like a miniature city. Only the city was a little schizophrenic. We had Boston brownstones down one street, Victorian mansions on the next. Gritty New York graffiti covered the walls of a pizza joint just around the corner from a suburban tree-lined street that could have been home to Wally and the Beave. Near the back of the lot were rows of squat warehouses where sitcoms and movies-of-the-week were filmed. And to the left was a colony of small bungalows that held the production offices of countless companies, all with cute little names from the Hollywood of old.

I'd done a little digging this morning on my cell while I'd waited at Starbucks and ascertained that Real Life productions was housed in the *Gone With the Wind* bungalow, which turned out to look nothing like antebellum Georgia. It was brick, short and had a faux-thatched roof that made it look like it belonged to a quaint English villager and not the biggest name in reality TV.

I shoved my sunglasses up on my head and was just about to knock on the door when a voice hailed me from behind.

"Excuse me?"

Uh-oh.

I turned to find a tall, dark haired guy standing behind me. He was dressed in jeans and a button-down shirt, untucked in a casual dressy kind of way. His square jaw, honey-colored tan and perfectly gelled hair screamed *movie star*, though his face didn't look familiar.

"Yeah?" I asked, doing my best Paris impression—fifty

percent valley girl, fifty percent bored to tears.

"How did you get in here?" he asked.

I cocked a hip and twirled a lock of hair, consciously dropping about 50 IQ points from my voice. "Waddaya mean?"

"Last I checked, Sunset was closed to reporters."

I froze, anxiety suddenly swirling in my gut. "Reporter? What do you mean reporter? I'm not a reporter," I lied, twirling furiously. "I'm Paris Hilton."

He grinned at me, a pair of dimples creasing his cheeks. "Oh, really?"

"Um, ya, really."

"That's funny."

"And why is that?" I asked, hating the way nerves made my voice about two octaves too high.

"Because you look a lot more like Allie Quick to me."

Uh-oh. Busted.

Chapter Four

"Right. Well, see, here's the thing," I said, quickly backpedaling. "What I meant was I'm here to see Paris."

"Paris is in Milan this week."

Great. The one day I don't check up on my celebrity itineraries... "I mean, I'm here to see a producer to talk about Paris."

"Uh-huh." Tall, Dark and Handsome crossed his arms over his chest and leaned back on his heels. He gave me a hard stare. "And who might that producer be?"

I puffed my chest out defiantly. "Alec Davies."

The corner of his mouth quirked up, and he shook his head at me. "Wow."

"What?"

The head kept shaking. "I knew tabloid reporters weren't the most truthful people on the planet, but you're kinda pathological aren't you, Allie?"

My turn to cross my arm over my chest. "I don't know what you mean." I paused. "And how do you know my name, anyway?"

That grin flirting with the corners of his mouth took hold in earnest as he answered. "I make it a point to remember the names of all the tabloid reporters who slander me."

Oh, no.

I felt a sinking in the pit of my stomach. "So...that would make you..."

"Alec Davies." He stuck a hand out toward me. "Nice to meet you." Then he gave me a wink.

If the ground could open up and swallow me whole,

now would be a very nice time for it to do so.

"Uh, hi." I limply shook his hand.

"Of course, I'm also known now as the 'shadowy figure' seen outside Barker's place," he said.

"I take it you read my article."

"Every last slanderous word. You here to interrogate your 'number-one suspect?'" he asked, quoting me again.

"I prefer the term 'interview.'"

He grinned widely again. I couldn't help but notice what a nice smile it was. His teeth were white and straight, dimples dotting both cheeks. It was a lot friendlier than I'd expect from someone using the word "slander".

"I'm not sure I want to be interviewed by you," he finally answered. "You don't exactly play fair."

"Are you saying you weren't outside Barker's the night he died?" I asked.

"I'm saying you didn't give me a chance to respond before printing your fairly unflattering article."

He had a point.

"Well," I countered, "here's your chance. Respond away."

"Touché." He grinned again, and I hoped he'd take the dare. "Okay, fine. Let's step inside, shall we?" he said, gesturing to the production office.

He didn't give me a chance to agree, instead pushing through the door and holding it open behind him for me. I followed, stepping into the small, three-room bungalow. A reception desk took up most of the first room, doors to both the left and right of the desk leading to the private offices. A guy in a plaid sweater vest and Ed Hardy sneakers sat in reception, talking into a headset. He did a little wave to Alec without missing beat in his conversation. Alec waved back then led the way through the door on our right.

This room was bigger, housing a large, modern chrome and wood desk in the center. A leather sofa sat against one wall, the opposite wall filled with built-in bookcases lined with DVDs. Several posters in sleek, black frames served as decoration, featuring TV shows I assumed Alec had worked on. A *Lady Justice* poster hung right above his desk, a girl in a lace teddy winking at me as she held the scales of justice in one hand.

"Have a seat," Alec offered, gesturing to the sofa as he took a place in the black, leather chair behind the desk.

I did, perching on the edge, knees together, legs on a diagonal to keep from flashing him a Sharon Stone in my miniskirt.

"So, shoot. Interview away," he said, leaning back in his chair, looking way too comfortable to be a killer.

I pulled a pad of paper and a pink gel pen with little hearts on it from my bag.

He raised an eyebrow at my choice of stationary, but said nothing.

"Someone was seen outside Barker's house at the time of his death," I said, pen hovering. "Wearing your ballcap."

"What cap would that be?"

"Black, red snake on the brim. From the *Lady Justice* set," I said, gesturing to the poster behind him.

"Ah. That cap."

"You admit you own one?"

He nodded. "At the risk of incriminating myself, yes."

"So, it was you?"

He paused. Then slowly countered with, "It was me who was at his house in a ballcap? Or me who killed him?"

"The former," I clarified.

"Yes."

"And the latter?"

"No."

Which, I noted, is exactly what he would say if he had killed Barker. "So what were you doing skulking around then?"

Those dimples made an appearance again. "I wasn't 'skulking,'" he said. "I was leaving. Through the front door. Down the front walk. Like a very non-suspicious person might."

"Leaving from?" I pressed.

"Barker and I were working late. We ordered Chinese in, had a couple beers, finalized a script, then I left."

Which was consistent with the ME report that Mu Shu Pork and Heinekin were among Barker's stomach contents. Though he'd ingested deadly levels of prescription drugs as well.

"And before you ask," Alec said, "no, I did not poison his beer stein. Now, that would be a very Agatha Christie twist, right?" He winked again.

I scrunched my forehead up, concentrating on being probing and not charmed. "What were you and Barker working on?" I pressed.

He shook his head. "Sorry, that's top secret. New show."

"Okay, what time did you leave?"

"Around ten. And, yes, Chester was alive and well when I left."

"Anyone able to verify that?"

He shrugged. "We were alone."

"So you were the last person to see Barker alive?"

"Actually the killer was the last person to see Chester alive," Alec pointed out. Then flashed that amused grin at me again.

"Why do I get the feeling you're not taking this interrogation very seriously?" I asked.

"I thought it was a interview." If it was possible, the grin grew wider.

"How well did you know Barker?" I asked, looking down to avoid his Charmorama.

He shrugged again. "As well as anyone, I guess."

"How long had you been partners?"

"About three years." He pursed his lips as if trying to remember. "But I worked for him for a few years before that. Chester gave me my first job right out of film school."

"As a producer?"

He laughed. It was a rich, deep sound that vibrated off the walls of his small office. Despite my detached journalistic integrity, I found myself instantly trying to come up with something witty to say just to hear it again.

"Hardly," he said. "I'd already hit every office in town, and no one was willing to hire a newbie. Chester took a big chance on me when no one else would. But he wasn't running a charity. I was green. I had to start at the bottom, just like everyone else. He gave me a position as a PA. Production assistant," he clarified.

I nodded, motioning him to go on.

"Anyway, I was basically a glorified errand boy that first season. But I learned the ropes and slowly advanced. Pretty soon I was working right alongside him, running the show for him."

"Running the show?" I asked. "I thought you were partners."

He nodded. "We were. Chester does the big-picture stuff, secured talent, locations, funding. I oversee the day-to-day stuff." He paused. "At least, that's how it was." For the first time since I'd sat down his jovial manner faltered.

As much as Barker had been known as the king of trash TV, it was clear that at least one person missed him.

"Do you have any idea who might have killed him?" I asked, softening my voice a notch.

Alec took a deep breath, blowing it out though his nose. "Look, Chester was a businessman. He'd be the first to tell you he was no humanitarian. He made enemies."

"What kind of enemies?"

He shrugged. "You name it."

"Any of these enemies ever threaten him?"

Alec nodded. "All the time. It was a slow week when he only got ten death threats. Last year he had to take three restraining orders out on former employees. And just last month someone stabbed him."

I leaned forward. "Stabbed?"

He nodded. "It was at our end-of-season wrap party for *Little Love*. Someone came up behind him and shoved a paring knife between his ribs."

I cringed. Ouch. "What happened?"

"One minute he's sipping champagne, the next he suddenly keels forward, yelling. I looked down, saw the knife, and called nine-one-one on my cell. A few minutes later the place is swarming with paramedics, and he's whisked to the hospital. He ended up being okay—the blade missed his lungs by half an inch. But he was sore as hell and hired a bodyguard to follow him when he went out in public after that."

A fat lot of good that had done.

"This bodyguard? Was he with Chester the night he died?"

Alec shook his head in the negative. "Chester figured he was safe enough in his own home."

Apparently, he'd figured wrong.

"So, back to the stabbing. I take it Chester didn't see who attacked him, huh?"

Alec shook his head. "No. The party was packed, and the guy came at him from behind." He paused. "Or girl. By the time anyone even realized what had happened, the attacker had disappeared into the crowd again."

"Chester didn't have any suspects then?"

Alec grinned, showing off his dimples again. I had to admit, I was having a harder and harder time picturing him as a killer. "I didn't say that," he said. "Chester had a list a mile long. He was a bit paranoid and thought everyone was out to get him."

"Apparently he'd been right at least once."

Alec nodded. "It's ironic how much pleasure he'd take in that."

"Who topped his list of suspects?" I asked.

"He was sure it was someone he worked with."

"Why is that?"

"Other than the fact Chester had no personal life? The party was on the studio lot, which means the public couldn't have gotten in." He paused, gave me a look. "Well, most of the public."

I ducked my head, ignoring the comment on my gate crashing. "So who was at the party?"

"Everyone who worked for RL Productions. All the cast and crew of our current shows."

"Which would be?"

"Well, like I said, we'd just finished shooting the first season of *Little Love*. We're getting ready to film the new season of *Don & Deb's Diva Dozen*, and *Stayin' Alive* will wrap up next month."

I wrote the show names down. "So, someone stabs Barker, but only wounds him. A couple weeks later Barker is poisoned. Same person?"

Alec shrugged. "You're the investigative reporter. You tell me."

Trust me, I intended to.

"Anything else you can tell me about Barker?" I asked.

"Just that you've got your work cut out for you. You didn't get to be in Chester's position by making friends."

I capped my pen, shoving it and the notepad back in my bag. "Well, thank you for the interview," I said.

"No problem. Just be nice to me in your paper this time, huh?" he asked then winked at me again.

I felt my cheeks go flush. "Sure," I mumbled, making for the door.

"See you around, Paris," he called after me, flashing those dimples again.

The way that grin made my skin go warm, I kinda hoped so.

* * *

The first thing I did when I got back to the office was pull up the Internet Movie Database (IMDB) to check out the list of shows Alec had given me. While the names were familiar, I wasn't exactly a reality TV devotee, and I needed the deets.

IMDB holds a list of every TV show and movie made in Hollywood, complete with the names of every single person who ever worked on it. Very handy if you were fishing for suspects in a very big pond.

Right off the bat, I eliminated the crew members low on

the totem pole. Besides the fact that they'd have very little day-to-day contact with Barker, at least according to Alec's description of his role, crew turnover was so fast in this town that I doubted any of them had had enough time to grow a murderous grudge against the producer.

Which left the cast of his latest reality hits.

I pulled up the name of the first show, *Little Love*, and read the description.

Little Love was a reality dating show, where one eligible bachelor was put into a house with twenty hot, young single girls. Every week the girls tried to out-flirt each other on group dates to earn a rose at the end of the hour-long show. The last one left standing at the end of the season got a proposal from the bachelor. To be honest, it sounded like any number of dating shows I'd already seen on TV. Except Chester added a twist to his. All the contestants on the show were little people. As in dwarfs.

I scrolled through photos of the little ladies, all dressed in evening gowns and having cocktails with the little bachelor, a guy by the name of Gary Ellstrom.

I looked at his photo. Gary had the typical features and body type associated with achondroplasia dwarfism—an elongated forehead and average-sized torso, coupled with shortened limbs. He had dark hair, dark eyes and wore a sparse mustache on his upper lip.

I wrote the info down on a post-it (pink and shaped like a heart), before moving on to the next show on my list: *Don & Deb's Diva Dozen*.

Anyone who hadn't been living under a rock for the past year knew Don and Deb Davenport. They were the parents of 12 children: two sets of triplets (ages six and ten) and a set of sextuplets (four-year-olds). Which in itself was enough to become reality show royalty, but Don and Deb took their fame one step further—all twelve of their children competed on the Tiny Tot beauty pageant circuit. They were in their fourth season, and the ratings just kept climbing.

Though, in all fairness, some of the recent rating hikes had been due more to Don and Deb's personal life than their children's painted faces and fluffy-pink costumes.

Deb's close-cropped hairdo had been plastered all over the tabloids recently (including our fair paper), ever since Don had been photographed with a string of young co-eds at trendy Hollywood nightclubs. Rumor was he'd had an affair, but no one had ever come forward claiming she was the other woman. At the beginning of last season the couple had announced a trial separation. Deb took the sextuplets, doing the Southern Glitz pageant circuit, and Don took the triplets, doing the West Coast Sunshine pageants. The separation had lasted right up until sweeps week, when the couple announced they were going to give marriage a try again. The season had culminated in an hour-long *Don & Deb's Reunion* show where the couple took all twelve children to Vegas for a long weekend, renewing their vows at the MGM Grand.

I wrote down Don and Deb's names, along with their dozen (Dorri, Diana, Delilah, Dolly, Daria, Donna, Daphne, Deirdre, Destiny, Dominique, Demitra, and Drea), though I doubted we were looking at a Tiny Tot killer.

Last on my list was the show that had put Chester's name on the map in the first place—*Stayin' Alive*. Currently in its ninth season, *Stayin' Alive* was the granddaddy of all reality shows, pitting fifteen strangers against each other to fight for the title of Last Survivor Alive. Each season, Chester dropped the contestants in the middle of nowhere, the only location requirements being a beach (where the female contestants could wear their teeny tiny bikinis), torrential rains (that wetted said bikinis suggestively), and lots of big, hungry mosquitoes (just for kicks). This season was *Stayin' Alive: Tonga*, and each week all fifteen contestants would brave both the elements and each other, fighting it out in reward and immunity challenges. Anyone who did not win immunity was forced to go to the tribal staging area, where someone was sent home each week. However, they weren't voted out on their survival skills.

Instead, the contestant participated in a dance-off, where a panel of judges voted out the contestant with the worst ballroom skills. We were three weeks from the end of the season, which meant the contestants still had to dance the cha-cha, the tango and, the grand finale, the Venetian waltz.

While I figured none of the contestants likely had much contact with Barker—being that he was killed here and not in Tonga—the three judges had been with him since the beginning of the show, giving them plenty of time to build up a grudge. Damon Crow, a record producer from Detroit, was the first, a big guy who tended to phrase his critiques of the contestants with so much slang they needed urban dictionaries to decipher his meaning. Mitzy Reed was second, an 80's pop icon just this side of being labeled washed-up. And just this side of sober most of the time. She had a reputation for being able to find something nice to say about even the worst dancer. Which nicely balanced out judge number three, Lowel Simonson, an Australian-born choreographer whose favorite word was "dreadful," followed closely by "horrendous" and "no-talent hack." Needles to say, America loved to hate Lowel.

After I wrote all three names down, I sat back and looked at my list of suspects. Twelve beauty pageant contestants, two on-again-off-again parents, twenty-one dwarves, and three reality show judges.

Oh boy. Alec was right. I seriously had my work cut out for me.

Chapter Five

I chewed on the end of my sparkly pen, doing an eenie-meenie-minie-mo over which suspect I was going to tackle first. I was just about to catch a tiger by the toe when a head popped up over the fabric partition of my cube.

"Hey, Allie," a six-foot-tall blonde said. "Watcha working on?"

Cameron Dakota, our resident photographer. She leaned over my shoulder, glancing at my pad of paper.

I quickly covered it. "Nothing."

"I heard you were on Barker," she pressed. "Any hot leads?"

While her tone was friendly, her motives were suspect. Cam had been friends with Tina long before I'd arrived on the scene, meaning if she had to pick, her allegiance lay with Tina every time. And she did have to pick. Every time.

I glanced across the newsroom at Tina's desk. She was engrossed in something on her computer screen. Maybe a little *too* engrossed.

I turned to Cam. "Tina sent you over her to spy, didn't she?"

Cam blew air out through her lips in a *pfft* sound and rolled her eyes. "No!"

I gave her a get-real look.

She bit her lip. "Okay, fine, yes." She looked over her shoulder once, presumably to make sure Tina hadn't caught her spilling the beans, then collapsed into the plastic chair beside my desk. "God, I hate being in the middle of you two."

Cam twisted a lock of hair between her fingers. Clearly she was not cut out to be a spy. Cam was a blue-eyed, blonde-haired, typical California surfer girl. A natural beauty, she rarely did the make-up or hairspray thing, going more for ponytails and lip balm if anything. The irony was, she'd recently started dating one of Hollywood's hottest movie stars, making every surgically enhanced wanna-be starlet in Hollywood cry "no fair". Honestly, I was happy for Cam. While she was often roped into being Tina's henchwoman, she wasn't really all that bad on her own.

In fact, when I first came on board, the tension between Tina and I had been immediate and fierce, drawing a clear line in the sand between us. Of course, me being New Girl, everyone on staff had fallen on Tina's side of the line. Which was fine. I mean, it would have been nice to have someone show me the ropes—or at least where the ladies' restroom was—but I didn't need any special favors. I knew I could get the stories all on my own.

But those first few weeks Tina might as well have been handing out T-shirts that read Team Tina, because no one would give me the time of day.

Cam had been the only person in the entire newsroom who'd even talked to me. Granted, she also wasn't vying for page space with me, but it had been nice not to be treated like a total leper. Since then we'd worked together on a couple stories, actually making a pretty good team. I wouldn't go so far as to say we were BFFs, but I generally trusted her.

Generally, that is, when Tina wasn't thrown into the mix.

"Sorry," Cam said. "She kinda roped me into coming to check on you before I could say no."

I shrugged. "It's okay. In Tina's place, I would have done the same thing."

"You know, I'm always amazed you guys aren't better friends. You're so much alike."

"Okay, now I hate you."

Cam grinned. "So, how are things coming with Barker?"

"Well…" I hedged, knowing anything I said was probably going straight to Tina. On the other hand, I didn't really have much more than a list of reality show actors anyway. So I showed it to Cam, giving her the brief rundown of the case.

Cam looked at my list. "Well, Don and Deb—pretty much everyone knows about them. They break up and get back together, depending on the ratings. Total dysfunction." She scanned down the list again. "I honestly don't know much about Lowel Simonson. He pretty much keeps to himself as far as interviews go. I know he's in town, though. I was doing LAX coverage last week and saw him arrive from Tonga."

Which was, conveniently, just before Barker was killed.

"Know where he's staying?" I asked.

Cam shook her head. "No. But word is, he'll be in town for at least a few days before flying back for the next judging round."

I wrote: *In town when B killed. Alibi?* next to Simonson's name. "Anyone else jump out at you?" I asked.

She looked at the list again. "This guy," she said, pointing to the Little Bachelor, Gary Ellstrom. "He's a real hothead. I was down at The Grove last week. Turns out he works in some boutique there now, and he totally cussed out some lady just because she wanted his autograph."

"Hot temper, huh?"

She nodded. "Oh, yeah. When he was on the show, they brought in some anger management therapist. Apparently he kept blowing up and breaking camera equipment."

"Sweet." I put a star next to his name, shooting him to the top of my list. "You remember the name of the boutique?"

She nodded. "Bella Sole. They sell designer shoes."

I wrote the name down. "Perfect. I could use an afternoon at The Grove anyway." I threw my notebook and a sparkly pen in my purse and turned to go.

Only, Cam was still sitting beside my desk, looking like she wasn't quite done chatting.

"Is there something else?" I asked, itching to get going. I had a four o'clock deadline to get my article in to Felix, and so far I had bubkis.

"Sorta," Cam said. She stood up and leaned in toward me. She lowered her voice. "Listen, I have to ask…"

"What?"

"Well…" She bit the inside of her cheek, chewing thoughtfully. "Look, I know it's really none of my business, but there's this rumor going around, and I…well… I just…"

Uh-oh. "What rumor?" I asked.

"About you."

"About me what?"

"Well, some people are saying…and I'm not naming names—"

I'd bet a million dollars it started with a T.

"—but, well, it's been hinted at that maybe…"

"Maybe what?" I asked.

"You and Felix are sleeping together."

Mental forehead smack. "I'm gonna kill her," I mumbled.

"So, does that mean you're not?"

"No! God, no."

Okay, there had been The Night, but that had been before he was my boss, before it would have gone from bad idea to completely inappropriate. It was ages ago. It was so past tense. As in *slept*. Once. And, technically, we hadn't even really slept much. And I was definitely not *sleeping*, present tense, with him now.

"No. Definitely not," I emphasized.

"Sure. Right," Cam said. Though I could tell she still had her doubts.

"We're not!"

"Okay, okay!" She held her hands up in defensive gesture. "I believe you."

"Where, exactly, did you hear this rumor?" I asked.

"Um, nowhere in particular. Around. Here and there."

I looked over the top of my cube. Tina was still engrossed in her computer, the back of her purple-streaked head hunched intently over her keyboard. She looked a whole lot like *here* and *there* to me.

"Great," I said, hiking my purse higher on my shoulder. "So now everyone thinks I'm banging the boss?"

Cam went to nod. Then paused. "Maybe our mailroom guy hasn't heard yet?"

"Fabulous."

"Sorry," she said. "I just thought you should know. And, hey, I'm glad it's not true."

"Right. Thanks."

I watched Cam walk away. Then glanced around the newsroom. Max Beacon, our obits guy, peeked around the side of his cube at me. Mrs. Rosenblatt, who did our weekly astrology column, stood at the copier with Celia, our office manager. They were both shooting glances my direction then quickly back down at their copies, pretending they weren't talking about me. Across the room one of our freelancers was talking to our summer intern, a pimply kid with braces. They both stared my way, and I thought I saw the intern wink at me.

I narrowed my eyes at the back of that purple hair.

That's it. This is war, Bender.

*   *   *

The Grove is a shopping center located between Beverley Hills and West Hollywood. It's an open-air affair, but strip mall it definitely ain't. This is a full block of the most prime retail real estate you could get, housing upscale boutiques, exclusive restaurants and gorgeously choreographed fountains. On any given day you might see Angelina Jolie strolling through Baby Gap, or Kat Von D dragging her latest rock (or road) star to Maggiano's Little Italy. This was shopping, Hollywood style.

I self-parked in the garage off Fairfax and window-shopped (wishing I hadn't seen those credit card bills yesterday) my way to the middle of the center where the directory said Bella Sole was located. It had a Grecian-style entrance, pillars flanking a window display with mannequins all dressed like goddesses. In three-inch heels. I felt my Visa do a little wistful sigh as I pushed through the doors, inhaling the scent of new leather and four-hundred-dollar pumps.

In the center of the room were two rows of plush red chairs, three of which were currently occupied by women who could have been on Real Housewives of Orange County (and maybe one of them was…it was hard to tell, but the brunette closest the door looked a little like Jeana Keough, with a smaller nose.). To my left and right were rows of white shelves, illuminated from below, filled with fabulous footwear.

I walked to a shelf and fingered a pair of iridescent pink kitten heels. Bella Sole was way too classy to display price tags, but I could tell by the way the supple leather gave way beneath my fingers that it was somewhere in the range of out-of-my-means, bordering on I'd-be-paying-off-the-loan-for-the-rest-of-my-natural-life.

"May I help you?" a deep voice asked behind me.

I spun around…

Then looked down.

Gary Ellstrom stood all of four feet tall, his hands clasped in front of him, an expectant rise to his bushy eyebrows.

"Um, yes. Please. I'd, uh, like to try these on in a seven," I said, figuring posing as a customer was the best way to garner a little info from our Little Bachelor.

"Ah. A wonderful choice. Just a moment while I find them in the back. Please, have a seat," he said, gesturing to one of the red chairs.

I did, sinking into the plush cushions as I waited two beats for Gary to return with a pink and silver box. He made a big ceremony of setting it down beside me, lifting the lid with flourish and unwrapping layers of pink tissue.

"Hey," I said, leaning in. "Don't I recognize you?"

Gary pulled a poker face. "I don't think so."

"I do. You were on that show."

He sighed. "Here we go again."

"That dating show, *Little Love*, right?"

He sighed again and sat back on his haunches. "Yep. That's me. The Little Bachelor."

"I loved that show!"

He narrowed his eyes at me. "Really."

"Yes, it was fantastic! The way they—"

But he didn't let me finish, instead putting his hands on his hips. "Fantastic, huh? Exploiting a man's romantic hopes while making us all look like a bunch of mutated freaks just for the viewing pleasure of Jane Couch Potato is fantastic, huh? You get a kick out of that, do you?" he asked, his voice rising high enough that the Real Housewives all stared.

"Uh, well, I didn't really mean—"

"You think making a mockery of little people is funny? Medical conditions are so entertaining? Maybe you should go yuck it up in a cancer ward!"

Suddenly I was pretty sure the rumors of him being a hothead where not exaggerated.

"Hey, calm down, pal. I have nothing but respect for little people. Look, I'm only five-foot-one," I said, standing up.

He narrowed his eyes at me.

I sat back down. "Yeah, okay, I know. Not the same thing."

"No. It's not," he said, shoving the kitten heel on my left foot with a little more force than was strictly necessary. I winced but kept my mouth shut. Obviously Gary's strong reaction to the mention of the show was proof I might be on to something here.

"If the show was such an exploitation, why did you agree to be on it?" I asked.

"Oh, the producers had a totally different spin when they pitched it to me, let me tell you. It was all about showing the world that little people are no different than anyone else. That love comes in all sizes. What a crock!"

"I take it that wasn't what the show ended up being."

"Hell, no!"

The brunette housewife jumped in her seat at his words.

But Gary plowed ahead. "The producers took every chance they could to make me look like an idiot. They even said I had anger issues, can you believe that? Me!"

"Shocker."

"Anyway, the whole dammed thing was rigged from the

start."

"Rigged?"

"Staged. Set up. Barker had a real loose interpretation of the word 'reality'."

"So, it was scripted?"

"Well, no."

"You were told who to give your rose to?"

"Not exactly."

"You were told who to vote off?"

"No."

"Then I'm not following the whole rigged thing," I admitted.

"Look, lady, ever heard of editing?"

I ignored the attitude, instead encouraging him. "Go on."

"What they filmed was real enough, but they edited the footage to sell the story the producer wanted to tell. Everything we said was taken out of context. I'd say something to one girl, and they'd make it look in editing like I was talking to someone else. They made me look like a total asshole! What the public saw was not what really happened, you know?"

I nodded. "Okay, so what really happened?"

"What really happened was that I was stuck in a house with twenty bimbo wannabe actresses. Like I was really gonna find love with one of them."

I thought back to the few photos I'd seen on IMDB. "You didn't look all that put out when you were in the hot tub with Mandy. And Tandy. And Candy."

"Well, I didn't want to hurt their feelings. I'm a sensitive guy," he said, putting one hand over his heart.

Uh-huh.

"Only now," he went on, "my love life is completely ruined, thanks to Barker."

"How so?"

"What are you, stupid? Weren't you listening? He told the world I was some hot-tempered little freak!"

I gave him a look.

"I do not have anger issues!" His face turned bright red, a vein just above his right eyebrow pulsing wildly.

Two Housewives grabbed their purses and scuttled out of the store.

"What about the woman you picked at the end of the show?" I pressed. "Didn't you propose to her?"

"Oh, sure. Only, turns out she was just on the show to launch her career as a country singer. She was no more real than Barker. And what's worse, I had to pay for that engagement ring myself! Barker said it would show the world how serious I was about Tandy."

"I thought you picked Mandy at the end."

"Whatever. Point is, I'm out two thousand bucks now and gotta works this crappy-ass job on commission as a shoe salesman. A fucking shoe salesman! I'm Al Bundy, for Christ sakes."

I sat back in my seat, scrutinizing him. "Well, it sounds like Barker got what he deserved then."

"Yes, he did."

"I bet you were pretty happy to see him murdered."

"Ecstatic. I threw a fucking party."

"Where were you the night he was murdered?"

Gary paused, narrowed his eyes. "Wait—what is this? Barker's people set you up to this?"

"No. I'm with the *Informer*."

"The tabloid? Great!" He threw his arms up in the air. "Just what I need. My face plastered all over some cheap trash."

"Hey! We are not cheap." I made no comment on the trash part.

"Look, I did not kill Barker," he said. "You can print that. If you wanna know, I was here. Doing inventory. The new line of Pradas came in, and I was busy cataloguing the whole fucking lot of them."

That was a pretty calloused way to talk about Prada.

"Anyone with you?"

"Jesus, what is this, the fucking inquisition?"

"You sure they did much editing on that show?"

He crossed his pudgy arms over his chest. "Look, you gonna buy something or what, lady?"

God, I wished. I looked down at the kitten heels currently caressing (yes, caressing…they were that good) my feet. In my wildest dreams I couldn't afford them, let alone reality.

"Sorry. They're not really my style," I lied.

Gary threw the box down on the carpet. "Fucking hell!"

Chapter Six

I left Bella Sole with a serious case of shoe envy and a serious doubt that Gary had killed Barker. For one thing, I had a hard time envisioning Barker letting Gary into his place for a late-night chat. Clearly the man was not Barker's biggest fan. Second, I couldn't imagine him being calm and collected enough to poison the producer. Poison required planning and finesse to trick the victim into ingesting it. Now, if Barker had been bludgeoned to death with a pair of six-inch heels, Gary would be my suspect numero uno.

However, just to be sure, I phoned Bella Sole, pretending to be an unhappy customer, and asked to speak to Gary's manager. He confirmed Gary was, indeed, doing inventory the night Barker was killed. What's more, his manager had been with him the entire time, providing an iron-clad alibi.

Which left me with one suspect ticked off my list, but not a whole lot to write about for today's article. I looked down at my watch. I had three hours left to find something scandalous enough to be printable. With the deadline looming, I moved on to the next reality show under Barker's belt: *Don & Deb's Diva Dozen*.

As any member of the paparazzi knew, Don and Deb lived in a large, Tudor-style mansion in Beverly Hills, a far cry from the modest suburban digs they'd inhabited when the show first started.

I had to admit, I'd had some sympathy for the couple when they'd first gone on the air with their brood. With a dozen kids, it was hard to make ends meet for the couple. Deb had been a night shift nurse and Don a computer programmer—not exactly the kind of jobs that could support twelve college funds, let alone a hundred and fifty diapers a day. In their position I totally would have jumped at the idea of TV documentary paying to follow me around for a while.

Only "for a while" turned into an entire season's worth of episodes, which turned into seasons two and three, which had turned into a media phenomenon, sparking debates over everything from the morality of selective reduction of multiples pregnancies (something, clearly, Deb and Don did not believe in) to the morality of parading little girls in skimpy bathing suits with fake tans across a stage for a panel of adult judges (something they clearly did believe in). The family had become overnight household names, going from John and Jane Everyman thrown into mega-parenting to celebrity status. During their separation, Deb's face had graced the cover of People no less than five times. And I was pretty sure Don had his own TMZ cameraman assigned to him 24/7.

Besides fame, the other thing the show had brought Don and Deb was cash. Lots of it, I decided as I pulled up to the heavy iron gates surrounding the dozen's compound. Beyond the gates a lush, manicured lawn yawned up to the large brick house, bordering on castle in both size and shape. To the right was a grove of trees, where twelve little play houses sat. It looked eerily like a scene from the seven dwarfs. If all the dwarves had a thing for purple and unicorns.

I pulled over to the curb at the bottom of the road and made a quick wardrobe decision. I grabbed my faux Christian Diors again, popping them up on my head, and added an extra layer of lipstick, going ruby red. I puckered in the mirror, wishing I'd put a little more eyeshadow on this morning. I smudged what I had as high into my eyebrows as I could. Not perfect, but it would do. I drove my Bug up to the security talk box installed at the gate and hit the button to speak, waiting a moment before a voice came on the other end.

"May I help you?" it asked in a prim British accent. I instantly recognize it from the show—Nellie McGregor, the dozen's nanny.

"Allie Quick," I said, looking down at my fingernails in a bored manner for the benefit of the security camera mounted at the corner of the gate.

There was a pause on the other end. Then Nanny McGregor came back. "I'm sorry. I don't have an Allie Quick on my schedule," she said, annunciating the word *shed-duel* in British fashion.

I pulled my glasses down, rolled my eyes, did some more looking bored. "I'm the new pageant coach? For Donna, Deirdre and Daria?" I said, quoting the names of the oldest triplets who were, as of last season, slipping in their ranking as they grew from chubby little toddlers to awkward little preteens.

Again, I waited while Nanny McGregor checked her schedule. I mentally crossed my fingers that a household with a dozen little girls in tiaras was as disorganized as I'd hoped.

Luck must have been with me today, as Nanny McGregor came back on the line a moment later. "Fine. Come up. I'll meet you at the front."

Yes!

A second later the system buzzed and the big iron gates parted, leaving me a clear path to the diva castle. I wound my car up the road, following the big circular driveway and parking just to the left of the front door. True to her word, Nanny McGregor was waiting for me out front.

I made a big show of grabbing everything I could from the back of my Bug and shoving it a tote bag (Honestly I had no idea what a pageant coach would do with a pair of gym shoes, a roadside kit and a handful of used Starbucks cards, but I figured they'd have a bunch of "stuff," right?). Then I wrapped a silk scarf around my neck, slid my sunglasses up onto my head and "floated" the way I'd seen Miss America do up the front steps to meet Nanny.

While the words "British Nanny" conjured up images of sensible shoes, starched informs and white hair worn in a no-nonsense bun, Nanny McGregor was about as far as away from that as possible. For one thing, she was young—at least a couple of years younger than I was. For another, she was hot. Like, scorching. She had long, thick brown hair that hung loose over her shoulders, slim legs a petite girl like myself instantly coveted, and curves that while not the waif look currently in vogue among runway models, spelled voluptuous and sexy to any man. I figured it was a good thing the dozen were all girls.

"Miss McGregor," Nanny said by way of introduction as I approached, offering her hand.

I gave it a firm shake. "Allie Quick."

"The girls are in the rehearsal room. I'll lead you to them," she said, turning crisply on her ballet flats and leading the way into the dozen's castle.

I stifled an impressed whistle as I walked through the doors.

The castle theme continued here as rich oriental rungs covered marble floors, a large crystal chandelier hung from the coffered ceiling, and the walls were covered in wainscoting below flocked wallpaper. It felt more like a museum than a home full of rambunctious little girls (And if you didn't think beauty queen girls were rambunctious, I dared you to watch episode twenty seven where Dori pulled out a chunk of Dolly's hair over a pink sparkly tutu. These girls were serious about their bling.).

"Are the girls' parents available?" I asked, following Nanny McGregor down a long hallway flanked by display cases. Each was filled with trophies, sparkling crowns and satin sashes—the fruits of their pageant wins.

"I'm sorry, did you need them present for the rehearsal?" Nanny asked.

"Uh, well, it would be helpful to speak with them about what they expect from the girls."

"I can tell you everything you need to know."

"Hmm. You know, I'd really rather speak with their parents. I, uh, may need them to fill out some liability forms," I lied.

"I'm sorry," Nanny said, shaking her head. "Neither Don nor Deb is available."

"They're not here?" I asked, my hopes sinking.

"Don is meeting with their publicist downtown, and Deb is just finishing up her book tour."

I nodded. Deb had written a how-to book on juggling parenting and pageants, which had quickly catapulted her to bestseller status. I heard her signing in Alabama had a line of housewives around the block.

Which was good for her, but not so hot for my interviewing plans. On the other hand…

I looked at Nanny McGregor. Sometimes the help knew more about what went on in a household than the owners. I had a feeling if anyone knew Don and Deb's secrets, she did.

I followed her down a flight of stairs to what might have been a basement at one time, but had been converted into something akin to a dance studio. One tall mirror covered the back wall, the floors were covered in polished hardwood, and an iPod dock sat in the corner, featuring speakers half the size of my entire apartment. Along the back wall were all manner of wooden props— including a giant yellow sunflower, a mini convertible car, and a pair of lollipops twice the size of my head.

Three of the girls stood in the middle of the floor, practicing posing in the mirror. All were identical, save for a pair of pink ribbons tied in Girl Number Three's blond bob. They did kissy faces, "queen" waves and booty shakes at their reflections. In front of them a line of dolls had been set up, each one with a paper nametag pinned to its shirt. A Bratz doll was "Jax", a Cabbage Patch with a lopsided haircut "Eden" and a Barbie missing one shoe "Kristen."

Pink Ribbons Girl must have seen me staring at them as she explained, "They're the judges in the Pretty Little Miss pageant next weekend. We're practicing impressing them."

"Ah." I nodded.

"Kristen is from the south, so she likes lots of glam," she explained, pointing to Barbie. "Eden is tough on talent and Jax…" She rolled her little blue eyes. "She's the wild card. If she's in a good mood, she can be your best friend. But when she's PMSing, honey, look out." She did another exaggerated eye roll.

I stifled a grin. The little girl had to be all of five.

"Girls," Nanny McGregor said, clapping her hands to rally attention. "This is Miss Quick. She's Donna, Deirdre and Daisy's new coach."

Pink Ribbons pouted. "I wanna new coach too."

"You're fine with Miss Jamie."

"But I wanna new one!" She stamped her foot, pursing her lips up so her cheeks pooched out like a chipmunk's.

"If you run and get your sisters, you can stay and watch," Nanny told her.

The little girl thought about this for a moment then seemed to come to the conclusion that it was the best offer she was going to get. "Okay," she finally said, turning and running up the stairs, ribbons flying behind her.

I grinned again. "She's adorable."

"Thanks," Nanny said, beaming like a proud mama. "She's been rather difficult lately. Though I can hardly blame her."

A little frown creased her smooth forehead, and I took the opportunity to pounce on it. "Why is that?" I asked.

"The show. The press. It's hardly provided a stable home life for the girls lately."

I nodded sympathetically. "I can only image how difficult it must be for them, living in the public eye like that."

"Yes!" she agreed. "The paparazzi are relentless. Just last week a woman from a tabloid actually followed the girls into the bathroom with a camera. Can you imagine?"

"Horrible." I cringed, hoping that woman wasn't Cam. "I suppose Barker's death must be upsetting to the girls as well."

Nanny McGregor shrugged. "We've tried to keep the bulk of it from them."

"Probably for the best," I agreed. "Do the police have any leads?"

Nanny McGregor shook her head. "Not that they're sharing."

"What about you?" I asked, feeling her out. "You must have gotten to know Barker during filming. Any idea who might have wanted him dead?"

She shook her head again. "No."

"I heard he was a bit hard to get along with."

She thought about this for a moment before answering. "He was all business. Not very touchy-feely, if you know what I mean. But I suppose that's what made him so good at his job."

"Did Deb and Don think he was good at his job?"

At the mention of her employers her demeanor shifted, her back going just that much straighter, her eyes emptying of emotion. "I wouldn't know what they thought of him."

Ah, but *she* definitely had thoughts about *them*. "How long have you worked for Don and Deb?" I asked.

"Since the last set of triplets were born. I've been with the girls since the beginning, really."

"It must be quite a challenge, keeping up with twelve little girls."

Her features softened, a smile playing at the corners of her eyes. "I enjoy every minute of it. The girls are darlings."

I looked over at the matching darlings. They'd abandoned the mirror and were now arguing over who got to wear the gold tiara.

"Don and Deb are very lucky to have you."

And just like that the softness disappeared again, a curt nod all the response I got. Clearly the couple was a sore spot for Nanny. I mentally rubbed my hands together.

"I suppose you've gotten to know Don and Deb pretty well since you've been working for them," I pressed.

She nodded. "I suppose."

"How are they taking Barker's death?"

She shrugged. "Business as usual. The show must go on."

"Right. Just curious…" I hedged, "Did Don and Deb get along with Barker?"

"They fought with everyone," she said. "That's what kept the show on the air."

Good point. "Did they have any particular issues with Barker that you know of?"

She narrowed her eyes at me. "Why do you ask?"

Uh-oh. Too far.

"Oh, no reason. I just want to know what I'm getting into—working for the family, you know."

She nodded, seeming to understand that concept. "I'll be honest, between Deb's book tour and Don booking their next public appearance, they hardly even have time to see their children, let alone me. I can't tell you what their personal feelings toward Barker were, but I do know the show was eating this family alive. This last season was crazy. Paparazzi, the media hype, the separation. And the children are the ones who suffered for it. Poor Demetra wet her bed for a week."

I nodded sympathetically. "Change can be hard for the little ones."

"You have children?" she asked

"A cat."

She gave me a funny look.

"But Don and Deb patched things up, right?" I asked. "I mean, she forgave him for the affairs, didn't she?"

Nanny McGregor nodded. Then slowly and carefully said, "Yes, they tabled their differences."

Hmm. Interesting word choice. One that led me to believe she knew more about those "differences" than she let on.

I leaned in a little. "I'm not trying to be nosey…" Total lie. That was exactly what I was trying to be. "But I have to ask. Are the rumors true? Did Don really cheat on Deb?"

She paused, her eyes assessing me, before the British nanny code of "speak no evil" kicked in. "I'm sorry, but I wouldn't know."

Like hell she wouldn't. The mere fact that she was closing tighter than Fort Knox told me she knew more about the alleged affairs than she let on. I narrowed my eyes at her. She was young, pretty and awfully available. Was it possible Nanny McGregor was the unknown woman Don had been sleeping with?

I wondered. It was bad enough for Deb's pride that the entire country knew her husband was sleeping with someone else. But if Nanny had been that someone, I'd bet my laptop it was only a matter of time before Barker found a way to exploit that into next season's sweeps. I could think of a few people who might not have been thrilled with that, Deb's name leading the list. Maybe Super Mom decided to head off the humiliation before Barker got the chance?

"What about the reunion episode?" I asked, switching gears. "Was it all for show, or did Deb really forgive Don's indiscretions?"

She shrugged. "It's hard to tell what's real and not around here anymore. All I know is that Don and Deb both agreed to sign on for three more seasons." She sighed. "As long as the girls are on the air, the money keeps coming in. Sad, really."

It wasn't until she said that that I realized something was missing. The camera crew. Usually every moment of the kids' lives was being filmed, yet from the time I'd walked in the door, I hadn't seen a single camera.

"I'm sorry—where are the cameras now?" I asked.

Nanny smiled. "Gone. Thank goodness. When Barker died, production on all of his shows halted."

Which meant less exposure for the girls...but also for Deb. "So, Deb's on a book tour, you said?" I asked.

Nanny nodded. "Yes, just finishing it up."

"Was she out of town then when Barker was killed?"

Nanny squinted her eyes, as if trying to remember the day. Finally she shook her head. "Actually, no. There was a break between her Dallas signing and Denver signing. She came home for the weekend."

Music to my ears. I tried not to grin as I asked, "I suppose the police have already looked into alibis for the family?"

She shot me a look.

"As a formality. I mean, they always do on *Law & Order*, right?"

"Yes, they did." She paused. Then added, "Not that they needed to. Every movement this family has made in the last three years has been caught on film."

Which might make for a screwed-up childhood for the dozen, but made my life a whole lot easier. I made a mental note to track down that footage and see just want kind of alibi Deb had on the night Barker was killed.

"So, shall we get started?" Nanny McGregor asked.

"Started?"

"With the lesson." She clapped her hands, summoning the girls over to us. I noticed that while we'd been talking, Pink Ribbons had reappeared with three older girls in tow. Three very sour-faced preteens ambled my way. I had a feeling Nanny was right; the show really wasn't doing their personalities any favors.

"Girls, this is your new coach. She'll be working with you on runway presentation," Nanny said, gesturing toward me.

I swallowed, nodded, did a little one-finger wave at the three of them.

They stared at me.

"Uh, okay, let's get started." I racked my brain, trying to remember some of the lingo from the Miss America pageants. "Uh, let's start with…evening wear?"

The bigger of the three blinked at me. "You mean beauty?"

"Right. Sure. Beauty."

"I'm wearing pink. And she's wearing hot pink. And she's wearing pale pink."

Great choices. Maybe these girls weren't so bad after all.

"Okay, let's work on your walks, then." I put a hand on my hip, swaying it to the left and right as I walked across the practice room. I thought I heard Pink Ribbons giggle at me.

I spun around. "You try now," I said, nodding to the three older girls.

They looked at each other. Then at me. Finally the bigger

one shrugged and put a hand on her hip, sashaying across the room.

This time I was sure I heard Ribbons giggle. And whisper to the Barbie judge, "I give her a three."

Chapter Seven

Half an hour later I finally escaped Pageantland, hoping I hadn't screwed up their girls' chances at Pretty Little Miss too badly. I drove straight to the *Informer*, using my voice program to type up my notes on Don and Deb as I drove. Not that I had anything more than vague theories at the moment, but I figured a few pictures of Nanny McGregor's legs, a couple of shots of Don looking smarmy at some club, and the public could put two and two together just as well as I could.

As soon as I hit the offices, I proofed the copy for typos then sent it through the *Informer*'s system to Felix's desk. I glanced down at my watch. 3:49. Was I good or what?

My copy turned in, I focused on hunting down the footage that could possibly condemn or exonerate Mom of Barker's death. I started by calling my very small network of informants to see if anyone could get me raw footage from the night Barker had been killed. Unfortunately the footage had yet to air, and was, from all I could gather, locked up tight at Sunset Studios, in a holding pattern now that Barker was gone and the future of the show uncertain. I talked to one grip, who knew an extra dating the third camera guy on *Don & Deb's Diva Dozen*, who informed me he thought he could get me a copy if I was willing to pay. Ten thousand bucks. Let's face it, my contacts sucked. And even I wasn't brave enough to spend that much of Felix's money.

Which left me with just one more alternative.

I picked up the phone and punched in the main number to Real Life Productions. A young guy with a distinctly San Franciscan accent answered, "RLP, how may I help you?"

"Uh, hi. Can I please speak with Alec Davies?"

"And who may I ask is calling?'

"Allie Quick."

"And this is regarding?"

I bit my lip. "Paris Hilton."

There was a pause on the other end, then a, "Please hold."

I waited a moment, listening to a musak rendition of "Love in an Elevator" before a familiar voice came on the line. "Paris, huh?"

I could hear the grin behind his words and pictured those dimples to go along with. It was a nice image. Nice enough that I felt myself blush a little, glad he couldn't see me. "I thought you'd enjoy that."

"So, Miss Quick, to what do I owe the pleasure?"

I pictured him leaning back in his chair, his voice casual, his feet up on his ridiculously expensive desk.

"I was wondering if I could ask you a teeny tiny favor."

"A teeny tiny one, huh?"

"Miniscule."

"I tell you what—you can ask. I can't promise to deliver."

"Fair enough. *Don & Deb's Diva Dozen*. I was wondering if I could have a little peek at the footage from the day Barker died?"

There was a pause. Then, "Why?"

Great question. But I figured I had nothing to lose by being honest this time. "I want to see if the cameras caught Deb's alibi for the night Barker died."

I heard leather on leather squeak as Alec shifted in his chair. "Again, I have to ask, why? Do you have some evidence that points to her in his death?"

"Evidence? No."

"A hunch?"

"You could call it that." I paused, unsure how much Alec knew about Don's affairs. "I couldn't help but notice life has become a lot less public for the family since Barker died."

"That's true," Alec hedged.

"Which could be a godsend when you're the butt of two out of three late-night monologue jokes."

"Good point." I could hear the smile in Alec's voice.

"Their new contract," I asked Alec, "what happens now that Barker is dead?"

"Their contract is with RLP, so technically it would still stand."

"Technically."

"Right."

"But in actuality?"

He sighed. "In actuality, the future off all our shows is up in the air. Look, I'm the first to admit, I'm a details guy. I can run a show like clockwork. But Barker was the creative force behind them all. Without him, I'm not sure we *want* to continue all the shows, let alone *can* continue."

"Which might leave those wanting out of their contracts, or out of the spotlight, a nice motive."

Alec paused. Then, "I'll see if I can dig up the footage. No promises, but I'll see what I can find."

"Perfect!"

"Always glad to help my friendly neighborhood tabloid reporter," he said. Then hung up.

I was still celebrating my mini-victory when I heard Felix's voice bellow from across the room.

"Quick!"

I jumped in my seat, spinning around to find him framed in his office doorway, staring at me, eyebrows drawn.

"My office. Now!" he said. Then ducked his head back in the door.

Uh-oh. Not good.

I took a two count to pull myself together (tugged my hemline down, fluffed my hair up) and pushed through the glass doors to find Felix at his desk, eyes intent on his computer screen.

"You got my copy?" I asked.

"Reading it now."

"Is there a problem?"

His gazed popped up. And immediately I knew there was. His eyes were an angry dark blue, his lips drawn tight, his forehead creased. "With the copy? No. With my credit card? Yes."

I cleared my throat. "Your credit card?"

"What the hell is a charge for a limo service doing on my account?"

"You got the bill already, huh?"

"Yes, I got the bill already! Tell me what the hell one of my reporters is doing gallivanting around town in a limousine?"

"I was hardly gallivanting," I protested.

"Allie…" he growled.

"I was investigating. I needed the limo to get into the

studios to interview Alec Davies."

The vein subsided slightly. "What do you mean, you needed it to get in?"

"They weren't going to let me in, so I pretended to be Paris Hilton. And she wouldn't very well drive a Bug with broken air conditioning, would she?"

Felix opened his mouth to say something, thought better of it then closed it with a click. "Very clever."

I did a mental sigh of relief. "Thank you."

"But very expensive."

"Which is why I used your card."

And just like that, the storm in his eyes was back. "Yes, I noticed that. Exactly what are you doing with my credit card?"

"I memorized the number. For emergencies," I confessed. "Which, clearly this was."

He opened his mouth to speak, paused, shook his head and settled for running a hand through his hair, making it stand up in little tufts. "Just tell me you got it."

"Got what?"

"The interview with Alec Davies? 'Paris' was allowed entry to the studios, I presume?" he asked.

"Yes, she was. And, yes, I did."

"And?"

"And Davies is not our killer."

"So he wasn't outside Barker's then?"

"Well, yes, he was actually."

Felix paused. "But he has an alibi for the time of the murder?"

"Um, well, no, not exactly. But he was gone by then."

"Gone?"

"He had dinner with Barker, went over some scripts then left. While Barker was still alive," I added.

"And we're certain he didn't sneak back in and off the fellow?"

I paused. "Define 'certain?'"

Felix closed his eyes and rubbed his temple as if a headache was brewing there. "Okay. So, tell me—upon what are we basing his innocence?"

I bit my lip. I was pretty sure the answer he was looking for wasn't a charming smile and a killer pair of dimples. "It's just a feeling," I finally settled on.

"Are you blushing?"

"What?" I ducked my head. "No."

"Huh."

I cleared my throat. "Anyway, I think Deb has a much more viable motive to want Barker dead."

Felix glanced at my copy on his computer screen. "Especially if her husband was, in fact, sleeping with the nanny, as you've so cleverly insinuated."

I couldn't help feeling just a little pride at the word 'cleverly'.

"Any idea if she has an alibi?" Felix asked.

"I'm working on it."

"What about Don?" Felix asked. "Any idea how he felt about Barker possibly taking the name of his affair public?"

I shrugged. "I'm guessing not so hot?"

"Don't guess. Find out," Felix ordered.

"On it," I said, making a mental note to track down American's favorite philanderer tomorrow.

"Good. Someone like you should be able to get him to open up easily enough.

I paused. "Like me?"

He nodded. Then looked at my boobs.

"You mean, a stacked blond?" I clarified, jutting one hip, planting both hands on it.

He sighed. "Look, you know as well as anyone that you've got to use what you have to get the story you need." He glanced down again. "And Don clearly has a thing for what you have."

I rolled my eyes. "Jesus, Tina was right. You really do think my asset to this paper ends in a cup size, don't you?"

"That's not what I meant."

"That's exactly what you meant. Tina uses her contacts, Cam uses her camera and I use my body. Gee, good thing I went to college."

"Hey, you're the one who just impersonated Paris to get into Sunset Studios," he pointed out. "What do you call that?"

I shook my head. "That's totally different."

"How, may I ask?"

"It...it just is!"

"Grand argument."

I clenched my teeth together. "*L.A. Times* reporters do not use their boobs to get a story."

"We are hardly the *L.A. Times*."

"Don't I know it!"

"Wait, are you dissing our paper?"

"Did you just use the word 'dissing?'"

"Don't change the subject."

"Trust me, I'm not. I'm totally on the subject of how I'm only a pair of measurements to you."

"On second thought, a change of subject isn't altogether uncalled for."

I threw my hands up in the air. "You know what? Forget it. I will get that interview with Don. I will get him to spill everything. And you know why?"

He bit his lip. "I'm not sure I want to at this point."

"Because I always get my story. Because I'm a damned good reporter. Too good for this place."

Felix opened his mouth to shoot back an answer, but I didn't wait around to hear it, having been insulted enough for one day. Instead, I stormed to my desk. Only that was right outside Felix's office, and I didn't quite feel like I'd stormed enough. So I stormed all the way through the newsroom to the stairs, slamming the stairwell door good and loud on my way out. I marched down the entire flight, shoving out into the assaulting sunshine. I got all the way to my car before I realized I'd left my purse in my cube.

Sonofa—

I closed my eyes, leaned against the hood of my car and thought about a million dirty words, most directed at men in general and a few choice ones directed Felix specifically.

I waited until I ran out of creative slams then slunk back up the stairs, mustering up as much dignity as I could, walking back through the newsroom and grabbing my purse from my cube.

I could feel Felix watching me from his office but didn't give him the satisfaction of turning around. Instead, I put blinders on as I marched back down the stairs again and out to my car, this time peeling out of the lot with an audible screech for his benefit.

* * *

I drove to the nearest Starbucks and ordered myself a venti Frappuccino with an extra vanilla pump, whipped cream and chocolate shavings. By the time I'd finished I had a hell of a sugar rush, but my anger had almost cooled down.

Almost.

I grabbed my gym bag from my car, slipped into a pair of pink yoga pants, a matching pink tank and running shoes then headed straight for the gym, grabbing the only available Stairmaster. As always, as soon as my body got into the steady rhythm of planting one foot after the other, the tension slowly drained from my limbs.

I loved the gym. I know a lot of women say they love going to the gym, but what they actually mean is that they love being skinny, even if it means they have to endure the torture of being at the gym three times a week. But I actually loved the gym. Being here was my form of meditation. When I was sweating on a Stairmaster, all I had to think about was putting one foot after the other. It was all physical, and my mental hamster could just sit down and snooze for awhile, zone out and let calm settle over my thoughts.

I did forty minutes on the Stairmaster then switched to weights, grabbing a fairly light set before settling myself on a giant exercise ball in front of the mirror. I lifted the weights above my head, working my shoulders, back and eventually abs.

By the time I was done my muscles were loose and warm and my mind a blissful blank.

I took a quick shower, towel-dried my hair and reapplied my makeup in the locker room mirrors. I hit the juice bar next door, ordering a salad and a smoothie, then grabbed a table near the back and pulled out my cell.

Despite my fight with Felix, I knew he was right about one thing—I needed to talk to Don. While poisoning was traditionally more of a woman's weapon, Don did have a pretty good motive to want Barker gone too. Especially if he really was sleeping with the nanny and planned to keep it quiet.

I pulled up my address book and dialed the number of Don's publicist. Official channels would be, as I knew, futile. I could beg the woman for an interview, but no publicist worth her salt would ever agree to one with a tabloid. Instead, my best bet was to find out where he'd be tomorrow and ambush him. So, when a receptionist came on the line saying, "Pfiffer media, how may I help you?" instead of Allie Quick, I put on my best Nanny McGregor voice, hoping my hours of listening to Felix's accent would finally work to my benefit.

"Cherrio, this is Nellie McGregor," I said.

"Yes, Miss McGregor, how can I help you?"

"I'm quite sorry to bother you, but I seem to have misplaced Don's *shed-duel* for tomorrow," I said, drawing out the word the way I'd heard her do that afternoon.

"No problem," the receptionist told me. "I can email you a copy."

"Uh…I'm not at home this moment. Would you mind sending to my cell?"

"No problem, happy to."

I quickly gave her my number then hung up and watched my screen. Two minutes later the text came in, outlining every place I could expect Don to appear tomorrow.

Unfortunately his day was packed tighter than Lindsay Lohan's court schedule. He had a meeting in the morning with some studio executives, a lunch date with his agent, a dinner date with his manager and an afternoon radio interview sandwiched between.

Considering the meetings were behind Sunset Studio's walls (and my Paris gig was getting a little old), I figured the best place to ambush him was at the radio show. I wrote the time and station down.

Pretty pleased with my day's work, I downed the rest of my smoothie and pointed my Bug toward home, glad to put this day to rest.

* * *

I awoke to the sound of pounding on my front door. Loud, insistent pounding. I rolled over and looked at my clock. Seven-fifteen. Ugh.

I dragged myself out of bed as the pounding continued.

"I'm coming!" I yelled, shuffling to the offending object and undoing the locks one by one. I pulled it open.

And looked down.

"About fucking time!" Gary Ellstrum stood on my doorstep, hands on hips, glaring at me. "Jesus, how long does it take a person to answer the door?"

"It's seven in the morning. What are you doing here?" I asked, ignoring his cheery mood.

"I'll tell you what I'm not doing today," he said, pushing past me into my living room.

"Please, come in. Make yourself at home," I mumbled.

"What I'm not doing," he continued, "is going to work. Wanna know why?"

"Not particularly."

"I got fired!"

"That's a shame."

"Guess why I was fired?"

"Do I have to?"

"Because of you! My manager heard me swearing at you and said I needed to get a handle on my explosive temperament. Can you fucking believe that?"

"Shocking." I yawned, muting the TV.

"That's it? That's all you have to say?"

I looked at Gary, now pacing, his face red, veins bulging. He looked like a shrunken, pink Incredible Hulk.

"Sorry?" I countered. And I was. Very sorry that he was pacing my living room at seven in the morning.

"Sorry don't pay my bills, blondie. I gotta eat. I have a very high metabolism. You know how much food for a guy with a high metabolism costs?"

I yawned again. "Look, I'm sorry you lost your job, but I'm not really sure what you want me to do about it now."

"I want you to hire me."

"Excuse me?"

"As your assistant. I looked you up. You do all kinds of investigating for that tabloid."

I shook my head. "Sorry. I'm not in the market for an

assistant."

"You need my help."

"What I need is sleep."

"I know stuff. Stuff that could be helpful to you."

I narrowed my eyes at him. "What kind of stuff?"

He shrugged. "Stuff. I'm very worldly."

I'll bet. "Look, in case the size of my apartment hasn't clued you in, I can't really afford an assistant."

He waved me off. "So, convince your boss. Pay me off as an informant. I know that paper of yours has money."

I bit my lip. It did. It also had a tight-fisted Brit at the helm who cringed when I expensed a three-fifty latte. I was pretty sure that after the limo charges yesterday, he wasn't going to see an assistant with anger issues as a necessary expense. "I'm not sure my editor will go for that."

"He will when I tell you who killed Barker."

I raised an eyebrow his way. "Okay, I'll bite. Who killed him?"

"Well, did you know that Barker was stabbed last week?"

"Yes."

"Oh." He looked disappointed, but he plowed on. "Okay, fine. But did you know this? Barker and Lowel Simonson were seen arguing that morning."

I leaned in. "Keep talking."

"They were heard shouting at each other in Barker's office. Then Lowel told him, 'I'd watch your back if I were you.' Pretty incriminating, considering he was stabbed in the back two hours later, huh?"

I had to admit, incriminating was a good word choice. "Where did you hear this?" I asked.

"I can't divulge my sources."

"Actually, if I'm going to print this story, you have to divulge. I need to check the facts. I can't print something uncorroborated."

He cocked his head at me. "You sure you work for a tabloid?"

I rolled my eyes. "Spill it, pal."

"Okay, okay, geez. Someone got up on the wrong side of the bed this morning."

I sent him a death look.

Luckily, Gary dropped it. "Look, after your visit got me fired, I had a little free time on my hands. So I called up one of the chicks from the show, Sandy, for a little recreational hot-tubbing, if you know what I mean."

Unfortunately I did. I held up a hand. "No details, please!"

He grinned. "Anyway, we got to talking about Barker, and she told me the production company screwed up her last check. So she was at the offices picking up a reissued one and overheard the argument between Lowel and Barker."

"And she's a credible witness?"

"Dude, she's a dental hygienist. You don't get much more professional than that."

I pursed my lips, staring at the little guy. I had to admit, it was a good lead. A great lead, even.

"So, am I hired?" he asked, his smile beaming under his sparse mustache.

"Fine," I finally said. But before he could celebrate, added, "for today. You can come help me interview Lowel. But that's as far as I can promise."

"Deal! Now, what are we having for breakfast?" he asked pushing past me into the kitchen. "I'm starving."

Chapter Eight

I showered and dressed while Gary cleaned my cupboards out of Captain Crunch and downed the last of my milk. As he toasted my last Pop Tart, I booted up my laptop. According to the Twitter buzz, Lowel was scheduled to shoot a Japanese commercial in Malibu that morning. After a quick call to the production company's L.A. office, pretending to be a P.A. who had lost her directions to the set, I had Lowel's exact location dialed in.

I grabbed my purse, notebook, and Gary and I headed for my Bug.

Only Gary took one look at my car and shook his head. "Uh-uh. No way. I'm not getting in that thing!"

I glanced at my car. "Why not?"

"Are you kidding me? It's a total girl car."

I rolled my eyes. "Of course. My mistake. Riding in a Bug might make your testicles actually shrink."

"Look, I got an image to uphold here. I'm the Little Bachelor. I can't be seen riding around town in that."

I put my hands on my hips. "So, what do you drive?"

He pointed to a suped-up Ford 150 with hydraulics that lifted the sucker a full five feet off the ground.

I grinned. "Compensation much?"

"Hey, that there is a man's vehicle."

"And this here is me leaving to interview our suspect," I said, turning over the engine. "You coming or not?"

Gary stared at me for a beat. Then he finally pulled open the passenger side door with a, "Fucking hell."

My thoughts exactly.

* * *

Lowel Simonson was known for being Australian, smug, and the biggest ass on television. His personal talent was coming up with comments that could build a contestant's hopes higher than the U.S. Bank Tower then shatter them to pieces all within the same breath. "That was the most amazing thing I've ever seen. Amazingly bad." Or "How long have you been taking dancing lessons? Because I think you should sue your dance teachers."

In college, my friends and I had played the Lowel Simonson Drinking Game, where we'd all gather to watch *Stayin' Alive* on Tuesday nights and had to take a shot of tequila every time Lowel said the word "pathetic". One week I got so drunk, I woke up on the dorm lawn. In my underwear. At 3 am.

As much as America loved to hate Simonson, they loved to tune in and watch him even more. *Stayin' Alive* ratings had broken every record that first season, and by season nine the number of people calling in to vote after watching Simonson rip contestants' dance moves to shreds had been higher than those who voted in the last presidential election. Twice over. I couldn't tell if that was a sad commentary on our political system, or a hopeful one on the entertainment business.

Thanks to his super-stellar ratings, Lowel was not only American's favorite asshole, he was also an international superstar. And while all A-listers knew that doing commercials for Metamucil and Swiffer products was as taboo as giving an interview to a tabloid, doing commercials for the foreign market was not only kosher but highly lucrative. Hence Lowel's current gig, pushing Happy Lucky Time toilet bowl cleaner to the tidy citizens of Japan.

Gary and I pulled up to a strip of beach just off the 1, where fifteen white trailers parked around a spot lit up by giant lights, white balloons, and white poster boards. In the center of the scene someone had placed a toilet on the beach, surrounded by a group of five Asian girls dressed in yellow go-go dancer outfits. Dozens of guys moved around them with cables, sound booms and camera tracks, getting the lighting just right to make the toilet sparkle with Happy Lucky Time shine in the California sun.

Normally location shoots were run pretty loosely. People milled around all over the place. However, Lowel Simonson wasn't your usual commercial actor. Being America's Asshole mean there were plenty of people with a grudge against the Aussie. And plenty of security in place to prevent said people from getting close to him. I counted at least five guys with

Tasers holding down the perimeter of the set.

"Great," Gary said, spying the security. "How the hell are we supposed to interrogate him now?"

"Interview. Not interrogate." I cased out the guards. The one farthest from the parking lot was the biggest. He was staring at a seagull with a potato chip wrapper in its mouth. He looked totally bored.

"Fine. How do we get an interview with him?" Gary asked.

"We ask nicely," I said. I grabbed a tube of lipstick from my bag and applied a fresh layer. Then I opened the top button on my blouse so that my lacy hot-pink bra was just visible beneath,

"Hubba, hubba," Gary said, eyeing my chest. "You plan to ask *very* nicely, huh?" He winked at me.

"Quit drooling." I got out of the car and walked toward Bored Security Guy, Gary a step behind me. When we were close enough that the guard's attention shifted from the seagull to us, I gave him a little one finger wave. "Hey, there."

"This is a closed set," he said, his voice a deep monotone like he'd already said this a hundred times today.

"Right. Totally. I know." I nodded. "But we're here to see Lowel Simonson. At his request," I lied.

The guard narrowed his eyes. "And you are?"

"Allie Quick."

The guard pulled a walkie talkie from his belt, inquiring of the person on the other end whether there was an Allie Quick on the approved set list. Obviously, there was not. Which he informed me as soon as his talkie crackled to life. "I'm sorry, ma'am, but we don't show an Allie Quick on our list."

I wrinkled up my forehead, bit my lip, my teeth making a dent in my uber-red lips. "Really? You mean he forgot to call ahead?"

"He?"

"My, um, booking agent."

"You playing a role in the commercial?"

I giggled. "Well, I'm playing a role for Lowel..." I leaned in close, making sure Bored Security Guard got a good look at my hot-pink lace. "... a private one. If you know what I mean."

He cleared his throat uncomfortably. Clearly he knew what I meant. "So, Mr. Simonson is expecting you?" he asked in a voice I'd swear was an octave higher.

I nodded. "Oh, yes, he is. And he'll be very disappointed if I don't show. See, he likes to relax a little before a performance." I winked at him. "I'm real good at helping guys relax."

His Adam's apple bobbed up and down.

"So, if you wouldn't mind just letting us slip on through to his trailer…" I trailed off, making my two fingers do a little walking motion in the air.

The guard thought about this for a moment, then shifted his gaze to Gary.

"Who's the little guy?"

I glanced down at my assistant. Good question. I pursed my lips. Well, in for a penny, in for a pound… "He's part of the act."

The guard's gaze shifted from me to Gary, back to me, then his two eyebrows headed so far north they almost cleared his hairline. Apparently this was way more info than he wanted about Lowel. He stepped aside, allowing us entry. "Just keep it in private, huh?" he said, giving Gary another over-the-shoulder as we made our way on set.

"Thanks!" I said, waving. "We will."

Gary giggled next to me.

"What?' I asked.

"Dude, that was brilliant! A couple of prostitutes. Ha!"

"Hmm. Thanks," I said, not entirely sure if I should be pleased with the complement.

"Seriously. I never would have thought of that. You are a good reporter, girl."

I cleared my throat, re-buttoning the top button of my blouse. "That wasn't exactly reporting," I mumbled.

"With moves like that, you must make the *Informer* a fortune. It's amazing your editor hasn't hired you an assistant until now."

I shot him a look. "Just leave the talking to me, okay?"

He put his hands up in a surrender gesture. "I'm a mute."

I should be so lucky.

"There he is," I said, pointing to where the actor in question was just emerging from one of the white trailers.

Simonson was average height, though he wore lifts in his shoes to tower over contestants on the show. He had dark hair, dark ominous eyebrows, and a spray tan that was always one shade darker than recommended. He wore his usual uniform of a white T-shirt and a layer of black jeans so form-fitting he had to walk with a sort of straight-legged hobble to the sparkling white toilet in the middle of the beach.

"Simonson's on the set," a P.A. announced, prompting grips and cameramen to scatter, putting their last-minute adjustments to their equipment.

Gary and I hung back, watching the director order everyone to "first position" and yell, "Rolling!"

Simonson did a pirouette in the sand then pointed to the toilet and said, "Happy Time Lucky makes the competition look pathetic." Then the go-go dancers sprang into action, giggling and prancing around him, until the director yelled, "Cut! Back to one!"

We watched the same scene a dozen times before the director was happy with his cut and the grips moved to set the stage for the next scene. The go-go girls lit up cigarettes, the P.A.'s sprang into action, and Lowel hobbled straight-legged to his trailer.

I elbowed Gary in the ribs. "Now's our chance."

I made for Lowel, catching up to him just as he hit the door of his trailer. "Lowel Simonson?" I asked.

He paused, hand on the knob, and spun around. "Oy. Who's askin'?" he asked, his accent markedly thicker than it was on the show as he squinted against the sun at me.

"Allie Quick. I was wondering if I could have a moment of your time?"

"For?"

Good question. "I'm…with a Japanese newspaper. We're doing a behind-the-scenes of the Happy Lucky Time commercial shoot."

"I thought it was Happy Time Lucky?"

"Right. Absolutely. May we come in?" I asked, gesturing to his trailer.

He looked from Gary to me then back. "You don't look Japanese."

"American correspondent."

He bit the inside of his cheek. Then nodded. "Yeah, okay. I suppose a minute won't hurt."

I did a mental fist-pumping "Yes!" as Gary and I followed Lowel up the two metal steps to the interior of his private trailer.

As we stepped inside, the décor was eerily reminiscent of the Winnebago I'd been forced to spend my eighth-grade summer in. A fold-down table jutted out from one side, a bench seat beside it. A pullout sofa took up one wall of the trailer, while a small kitchenette sat at the back.

Lowel lowered himself slowly (as a concession to his tight pants) onto the sofa, gesturing for Gary and I to do the same. "Please, sit down. Would you like some tea? Cookies? Lemonade?"

Gary and I looked at each other. This was America's Asshole?

"Uh, no thanks," I said, passing on refreshments as I took a seat on the edge of his sofa.

"You sure? They delivered a whole bunch of pastries to me fresh this morning. I have raspberry croissants?"

What was the catch? Was this like the tiger offering the wildebeest a salt lick before devouring her?

"Um, no. Thank you."

"Is it too warm in here?" Lowel asked. "I could turn up the AC?"

"I'm fine. Thanks. Listen, we wanted to ask you a couple questions about Chester Barker."

"Barker?" Lowle asked. "What does he have to do with Happy Time Lucky?

Good question. "Uh… he's very big in Japan," I hedged. "And our readers will be interested in what anyone who knew him personally might have to say about his death."

"Tragic," Lowel said, seemingly satisfied with my loose connection. "He was taken from this world too soon."

"You were close?" I asked.

Lowel shrugged. "I'd been working for the man for nine years. I was as close to him as he let anyone get, I'd say."

"Then how come you stabbed him?" Gary piped up beside me.

I elbowed him in the ribs.

"Ow! Watch the head!"

Okay, I'd tried to elbow him in the ribs, but he was a bit

shorter than I'd aimed for, hitting him somewhere in the temple region instead.

"I'm sorry, stabbed?" Lowel inquired.

"What my assistant meant to say," I quickly covered, "was that we recently learned Barker was stabbed a week before he was killed."

Lowel nodded. "Yes, I heard about that."

"You heard? You mean, you weren't there at the party when it happened?"

"Yes, I was. What I meant to say was that I didn't witness the incident firsthand. I was there when paramedics arrived and heard what happened then."

"So you admit you were at the scene of the crime," Gary said, pointing a chubby finger Lowel's way.

I shot him a look. What happened to my mute?

But Lowel just nodded. "I was. As was just about everyone who knew Barker."

"But not everyone had just been overheard arguing with Barker," Gary pressed.

"Yes, I'll admit we argued. But Barker argued with everyone he knew. It's unfortunate timing that we had a disagreement just before his death, but that's all it was."

"What was the disagreement about?" I asked.

"Business."

"What kind of business?"

Lowel fidgeted. "You sure no one would like a pastry? As I said, they're quite fresh."

"No, thank you. Now, that business—"

"I have orange juice to go with it. Fresh-squeezed."

"I'm fine. But the bus—"

"What about a coffee? I can have someone run to Starbucks for us?"

"Okay, enough with the nice-guy act," Gary piped up beside me.

Lowel blinked. "Excuse me?"

"You know, the polite-host thing to distract us from questioning you. I know it's all an act. 'Cause on the show, you're a total ass."

"Gary!" I hissed. So much for finessing our suspect.

But Lowel broke into a grin and let out a loud bark of laughter. "Oh, aren't you a card. Look, that's all for the cameras," he said. "Damon's the cool guy, Mitzy's the nice guy, and I'm the bad guy. It's just a role. Barker said it gives the show an edge, and I agree, the role's been very good to me."

"So you're a sheep in wolf's clothing?" I asked.

Lowel grinned again. "I like that. Yes, I suppose I am."

"You know what? Maybe I will have one of those raspberry croissants then," Gary said.

I shot him a look.

Lowel uttered a, "Splendid!" then pulled a tray of pastries from the kitchenette.

"As I was saying…" I said, steering us back to the conversation at hand. "The business you and Barker were arguing about before he died. What was it?"

Lowel passed the pastry tray to Gary then lowered himself onto the sofa again with a sigh. "All right, I might as well tell you. I'm sure it will become public knowledge soon enough anyway. My contract with the show was up, and Barker didn't want to renew."

"He was firing you?" I asked, hardly believing it. Lowel *was Stayin' Alive*. I couldn't imagine the show without him.

Lowel cringed. "Firing is such a nasty word. It was more like he was strongly suggesting that I retire."

"But why?" I asked. "I thought last season had the highest ratings ever."

Lowel nodded. "It did. Which was a blessing and a curse. Barker said the show needed something new and fresh to stay on top next season. His exact words were that our 'shtick was getting old.'"

"Meaning, *you* were getting old," Gary asked.

Lowel nodded, looking down at his hands. "He didn't say it in so many words, but yes, that was what he was inferring. Our target demographic is sixteen to twenty-two year olds. Just between you me and the walls, I'll be turning fifty-one this summer."

I gave the guy a good look. Now that he mentioned it, I could see the lines on his spray-tanned face and the distinctly gray roots peeking out of his dark hair. I wondered…

Lowel had a pretty sweet gig going with *Stayin' Alive*. If they brought someone new on the show, there went not only his per episode millions, but also his foreign commercials. Was he really willing to go out to pasture so docilely?

"Witnesses say they heard you threatening Barker," Gary repeated.

Lowel sighed again. "I said a lot of things to Chester I wish I could take back now."

"You told him to watch his back. And then he got stabbed. In the back," Gary pointed out.

Lowel shook his head. "Like I said, unfortunate coincidence."

"Can anyone vouch for where you were when Lowel was stabbed?"

"Well… I…don't know."

"So you have no alibi?" Gary pressed.

"What? No! No, I don't know. I mean, yes, I have an alibi."

"I thought no one could vouch for you?"

Lowel narrowed his eyes at Gary. I could see his sheep's clothing slipping a little. Then again, I was beginning to suspect Gary could've driven Mother Teresa to kill.

"Look, I did not harm Chester," Lowel said. "He was friend. We had a business disagreement, but I was sure my lawyers would think of something to keep my contract valid."

"And did they?" I asked. "Did it get resolved before Barker was killed?"

Lowel paused. Then shook his head. "No." His eyes took on a sad look, casting downward. Though whether his unhappiness was over his friend's death or the fact that he hadn't gotten his contract renewed, I'd be hard pressed to say.

"The night that Barker was killed, where were you?" I asked.

Only this time, the sadness had taken the fight out of him. "At home."

"Alone?"

He let out a short laugh. "My dear, in case you haven't noticed, I am never alone. I had security on site with me, who I'm sure can vouch for my movements."

I narrowed my eyes. Considering their livelihood depended

on Lowel not being in jail, I wasn't sure how reliable an alibi they really were. "Thank you for your time, Mr. Simonson," I said, rising.

He nodded, though he didn't get up to show us to the door. Instead, he grabbed a raspberry pastry, shoving it in to his mouth.

"So, do we believe him?" Gary asked once we were back in the assaulting sunshine.

I pulled a pair of sunglasses from my bag and put them on as we walked back to the car. "Hard to say. Confessing he was about to be fired because he's an old fart seemed pretty honest."

"Then again, maybe he's being honest about that to throw us off the fact that he really did kill Barker."

I nodded. "It's possible."

"And don't forget, he didn't give us an alibi for the time of the stabbing."

"Yeah, speaking of which," I said to him as we got back in the car. "Real suave interviewing technique back there."

"What? How do you conduct an interrogation?"

"*Interview*. And I find that if I start an interview calling someone out as a murderer, they're not real cooperative afterward."

Gary shrugged. "I prefer the element of surprise."

"Clearly."

"So, now what, boss?" he asked as we pulled back onto the PCH heading south.

Luckily I was saved answering by the sound of my cell trilling from my purse. I fished it out, popping my hands-free earbud in before answering. "Hello?"

"Allie? Hi, it's Alec Davies."

I have no idea why, but at the sound of his voice I felt a flush hit my cheeks and really wished my air conditioner worked. "Hi, Alec. How are you?"

"Great. Listen, I got hold of that footage you were looking for of Don and Deb."

"You rock."

I heard him chuckle in response.

"Where can I pick it up?" I asked.

"Well, actually, I was thinking I could deliver it in person to you. Say, tonight over dinner?"

I paused. Dinner? As in, a date?

"Oh. Uh, um, sure. Yeah, I guess."

"That is, if you're interested. I mean, tabloid reporters do eat, right?"

"Yes. I mean, yeah, I'd love to."

"Are you blushing?" Gary asked beside me.

I elbowed him in the temple again.

"Ow! Quit it!"

"What was that?" Alec asked.

"Nothing. Annoying bug. Anyway, yes, I'd love to have dinner with you."

"Great. How do you feel about Italian? There's a new place on Melrose I've been wanting to try? Mangia?"

I nodded. "Yep. Italian is good."

"Great. I'll text you the address, and we can meet there. Say, eight?"

"Perfect. See you then."

"Looking forward to it," he said then hung up.

"Who was that?" Gary pressed.

I cleared my throat. "A suspect."

"Dude, you have a crush on a suspect?"

"I do not have a crush!"

"You're blushing and grinning like you're thinking about getting laid."

"I am not!" I yelled, feeling myself blush even harder. "Look we're just meeting for dinner tonight so he can give me some alibi footage."

"Dinner," Gary repeated. "As in a date."

"Shut up."

"Oh, yeah. It's a date."

I opened my mouth to ask him how he'd like to be fired twice in one day, but I didn't get the chance. Instead, something hit us from behind, launching the car forward and jolting us both roughly against our seats belts.

"What the...?" I looked in the rearview mirror. Behind us was a big, black Escalade, the windows tinted so that I could just barely make out the form of a driver behind the wheel—though whether he was black white, male or female, I had no idea.

All I could tell you was that he was speeding up. Gunning right for the tail end of my Bug again.

Chapter Nine

I felt whiplash jolt through my body as the Escalade rammed my back bumper again. Both Gary and I surged forward, Gary popping up in his seat like a jack-in-the-box.

"Sonofabitch!" he yelled. "What's that guy doing?"

I didn't answer. I thought it was pretty clear what he was doing. He was trying to run us off the road.

I looked in the mirror again as he backed off, putting a few feet of distance between us. Then a second later, he surged forward, his grill bearing down on us.

Gary gripped the side of the door, his knuckles going white as he braced for impact. I did the same, holding the steering wheel in a death grip, sincerely hoping my airbags weren't as worn out as my AC. I quickly swerved to the right as he approached, causing his hit to glance off the right side of my bumper. The car swerved, skidding right. I tugged at the wheel, pulling to the left, just narrowly avoiding the bushes at the side of the road.

The Escalade hung back again, still following us.

"Do something!" Gary yelled.

"And what exactly should I do?" I yelled back. We were on the PCH between Latiago Canyon and Pepperdine U. There were precious few places where we could turn off. To the right sat the Pacific Ocean, to the left the sheer face of a cliff. The guy in Escalade had us cornered. And by the way he was biding his time, I had a feeling he knew it.

"Go faster!" Gary yelled.

For lack of a better idea, I did. I shoved my foot down on the gas, watching the gauge on my dash climb to 70 miles per hour, then 85. Once it hit 90 the car started shaking.

And the Escalade was still hot on our tail. Moving closer, coming in for the kill.

I watched him approach, one eye on the curve in the road ahead of me and the other on his headlights, growing closer and closer in the rearview. If he rammed us here, we were likely to go flying into the ocean. Unfortunately, I had a bad feeling that was exactly his plan.

"Holy shit, we're going into the ocean," Gary screamed

beside me.

"Not if I can help it," I mumbled under my breath.

I watched the Escalade approach, heard the sound of his motor revving, the big black monster barely breaking a sweat to catch up to my little Bug as she gave all she had. I waited until the Escalade's bumper was inches from mine and gripped the wheel with both hands. I held my breath. Then I swerved left as hard as I could, slamming on the brakes.

The Bug spun sharply into the lane of oncoming traffic, narrowly avoiding a Beemer as it zipped past us. The sound of his horn mingled with the screech of my tires. Smoke rose from the asphalt around us. Gary whipped right, his head slamming against the side of the car with a loud thud. I struggled to maintain control of the car, winding up facing completely the opposite direction as the Escalade sped past us, going too fast to stop. Through the mirrors I saw it disappear out of sight around the curve.

Then I didn't waste any time, stomping down on the gas pedal as hard as I could, tires spinning again. We raced back toward Malibu. Frankly, I didn't care where we were going, so long as it was away from that SUV.

Gary and I sat in adrenaline-fueled silence, our heavy breath the only sound filling the car. My hands gripped the wheel so tightly I feared it might take the Jaws of Life to pry them free.

It wasn't until we reached the next exit and I pulled off, tucking the Bug in the parking lot behind a roadside gas station, that either of us dared to breathe again.

"Holy hell, I think that guy was trying to kill us!" Gary said, his hand to his forehead where a large, red goose egg was forming.

"You okay?" I asked, my hands still glued to the wheel.

Gary nodded. "Kinda. Man, what an asshole!"

My thoughts exactly.

"Wow, you really must have pissed someone off," Gary said.

I spun on him. "Me? What makes you think he wasn't after *you*?"

He rolled his eyes. "Uh, duh! 'Cause we're in a lime-green chick car."

He had a point.

I leaned back in my seat, slowly prying one finger at a time from my steering wheel, flexing the tension out of them.

It was a pretty uncomfortable feeling, knowing someone out there wanted you dead. Or at least maimed. To be honest, I wasn't used to having any real enemies. I mean, it's not like our paper exposed political crimes or hardened criminals. My last assignment was Pippi Mississippi's hair color, for crying out loud. Occasionally a drunken celebrity would take a swipe at our cameras, but actual planned attempts on our lives were not everyday occurrences.

Which meant it had to have been someone connected with the Barker story. Someone who didn't like where my line of questioning was going. Which was both exciting (I must be on the right track, right?) and disconcerting (because I was still too far down that track to see the killer's identity at the end).

Had Lowel sent one of his bodyguards after us? Had Don or Deb gotten wind of my visit and hired a goon to run me down? For that matter, had one of them been in the car? It didn't take any special skills to ram someone from behind.

"I don't suppose you got a look at their license plate number?" I asked Gary.

He looked at me like I'd grown a second head. "Seriously? I'm lucky I didn't shit my pants."

Ditto.

I pulled open the car door and stepped outside, stretching the rest of the adrenaline out of my limbs as I walked around back and surveyed the damage to my car. It looked like someone had taken a sledgehammer to my back bumper. It was dented in about fifteen different places and hanging askew, as if it might lose its precarious hold any second.

"Poor Daisy," I sighed.

"Who's Daisy?" Gary asked, coming out of the car to stand next to me.

"My car."

Gary blinked. Then shook his head. "You are so girly."

I narrowed my eyes at him. "I'm a girl. I'm supposed to be girly. So I'm going to take that as a compliment."

He shrugged. "Your prerogative."

I ignored him, instead topping poor Daisy's tank off with gas. I went into station and bought a bag of Lays and a Diet Coke. I used the restroom. Checked the air in my tires. Generally wasted time being a big fat chicken about getting back on the road again.

"I'm bored," Gary whined, leaning against the hood of my car, sucking on an Astro Pop. "And my head hurts. Can we go home now?"

I looked down at my watch. 1 o'clock. In an hour Don would be finishing up his radio interview at KNLA. If I was going to head him off, I had to get on the road.

I took a deep breath, telling my inner coward that Mr. Escalade was long gone by now. "Yeah. Fine. Let's go."

We hopped back into my Bug and headed back up the PCH. At a slow crawl. Watching the rearview for any sign of menacing death vehicles. We both let out dual sighs of relief once we merged off onto the 2, back into smog-protected civilization.

I dropped Gary off at my place and watched as a set of steps popped out from the bottom of his truck, allowing him to climb into the Compensationmobile. I waited until he'd pulled away from the curb and turned the corner before popping back into Daisy and gunning it toward the freeway.

The KNLA studios were located north of L.A. proper, in Studio City. Just this side of the hills, Studio City was your first stop on your way into The Valley, a still-chic buffer between the exclusive Hollywood Hills and the bowels of North Hollywood. I took the 134 west until it merged into the 101 then hopped off at Laurel Canyon, heading south until I hit Ventura.

I pulled into a wooden complex with a subdued sign on the front, hidden behind a pair of mature palms. Unlike TV or film, radio was pretty much at the bottom of the entertainment food chain in Hollywood, which meant nary a security guard was present in the parking lot. Just the way I liked it. I parked in a slot near the back and set up camp to wait for Don.

I flipped on the radio, tuning in to KNLA. Immediately the interior of the car filled with the deep baritone voice of Bryan Crestor, KNLA's top DJ.

"Once again we're talking with Don Davenport, of *Don & Deb's Diva Dozen*. Don, thanks for being with us today."

"My pleasure, Bryan," Don's voice answered back. It wasn't quite as deep as the DJ's, and more nasally.

"So, we were talking about the difficulty of a man attending tiny tot pageants. How has this affected your life?"

I closed my eyes, listening to the DJ ask banal questions and Don answer with just as banal answers, while I mentally calculated a much more interesting set of questions myself. I knew the radio show was on a five-minute delay, so as soon as I heard the DJ say, "Well, we're almost out of time, but we'll take one more caller," I snapped to attention, scanning the front of the building for Don to emerge.

Two minutes later, he did.

Don was average height, growing a little stocky, as people with kids tended to do when existing on a steady diet of Happy Meals and mac-n-cheese. But he was fighting the suburban dad look with all he was worth by wearing an Ed Hardy shirt in a tiger design. In pink. Studded with sequins. He'd paired it with artfully acid-worn blue jeans, sneakers and a porkpie hat. He wore a book bag slung over one shoulder, making him look like an over-the-hill college student.

I bolted from the car, catching up to Don as he fumbled with a key fob at the door of a shiny, new Lexus.

"Don Davenport?" I asked, bearing down on him.

He looked up and tentatively answered, "Yes?"

"Allie Quick," I said, shoving a hand at him. "L.A. *Informer.*"

He narrowed his eyes, glared at my proffered hand then took a step back. "Nuh uh. No way. I saw that article you printed about me this morning."

"I take it you weren't a fan?"

"Are you kidding?" he sputtered. "You basically accused me of sleeping with my kid's nanny!"

"Well, technically, I just inferred it might be possible. I'm pretty sure I never accused. Legal wouldn't have let that run."

His eyes narrowed again. "Technical or not, she was in tears this morning. What if the kids read that?"

While I could understand his irritation, I highly doubted his kids had a subscription to the *Informer*. "Would you like to comment on the article?" I asked. "I'd be happy to print your response."

Don shook his head and crossed his arms over his chest. "No. Comment."

I sighed. I hated it when they did this. "Look, Don. I'm going to print something about you today, whether you like it or not." He opened his mouth to speak, but this time I ran right over him. "And we both know you've been in every tabloid in town, that the 'no comment' thing is bullshit, and that you're dying to comment and have your picture in our paper again, because if you're not in the tabloids no one remembers your name, and that's not the way to high ratings, is it?"

His eyes narrowed so far I wasn't sure he could still see out of those suckers.

"Now," I continued, "you can either answer my insinuations, or I can print up a whole new slew of them. I'm very creative."

He took another step backward. "Like what?"

"Like you stole that outfit from your daughters' closet."

He immediately looked down at his outfit. "This is a two-hundred-dollar T-shirt."

"Which makes it that much more of a tragedy."

He bit his lip, clearly not sure what to do with this situation.

"Look," I said. "I don't want to print that. I'm not a bad person. I just want an interview, okay?"

Don looked down at his shirt again. Then back up at me. "Fine. You win. But make it quick, I've got a thing with my manager to get to."

I gave myself a mental high-five. "Let's start with your affair. My story about it being with Nanny McGregor—was I close to the mark?" I asked.

"No!" He shook his head, a frown brewing between his eyebrows. "Absolutely not. God, she's my kids' nanny for crying out loud."

"Yeah, and guys never sleep with their kids' nannies. Unheard of."

But he ignored my sarcasm, instead still shaking his porkpie back and forth. "Look, if you knew our nanny at all, you'd know how ridiculous that is. She's totally focused on the kids. Jesus, sometimes I think she's a better parent than I am."

Damn. And I'd liked that theory so much. "Okay, so you weren't sleeping with the nanny. Who was it then?"

"Sorry, I can't tell you that."

"But you were having an affair?"

He nodded. Slowly.

"Chester found out who it was."

Don paused. Then nodded again.

"Where were you the day he was killed?"

"Whoa." Don jumped back, putting his hands up in a surrender motion. "You don't think I had anything to do with his death, do you?"

"Chester knew the secret identity of your affair. Exposing her at the next ratings sag would have been just his MO. Only he dies, filming stops, and your secret is safe. Sounds like excellent motive to me."

"No way!" Don shook his head so hard I feared he was going into convulsions. "Look, you've got it all wrong. That's not how it was at all."

"Then enlighten me. How was it?"

Don shifted from foot to foot. He bit the inside of his cheek.

"I gotta print something," I reminded him.

"Okay, fine. Look, I'll tell you. But this is strictly off-the-record."

"Fine. Off the record."

Don sighed. Looked over both shoulders. Leaning in close, he whispered, "I didn't have an affair."

I snorted. "Please. Every tabloid in town has footage of you out with hot young girls."

"Staged. All of it."

I cocked my head to the side. "Why on earth would you stage looking like a cheating ass?"

Don sighed. "Barker thought it was a good story to float. So he hired actresses to be seen out with me. God, you really think if I was having an affair I'd be that stupid to be photographed by every tabloid in town?"

Actually, he had a good point. And, with the exception of his wardrobe choices, Don didn't strike me as particularly stupid.

"So, the whole separation thing was fake?"

He looked down at his sneakers. "No, that was real

enough."

"I'm not following. Why did Deb want a separation if you didn't have an affair?"

"Deb didn't want the separation. I did." He paused, did some more examining of his over-priced sneakers then finally said, "Because she was the one who had an affair."

"Shut the fridge! You're kidding?"

"I wish I was."

"Details. What happened?"

He let out a long breath, sagging against the side of his car. "Look, it wasn't entirely her fault. We'd been growing apart for months. The demands of the girls were hard enough to handle. But then the cameras constantly followed our every move, catching every little disagreement we had and blowing it into a media sensation. It was all a lot to live with."

"And so she cheated on you?"

He nodded.

"How did you find out?"

Don took his hat off, running one hand through his sparse hair. I could tell he'd recently had plugs, moving his hairline forward a good three inches. "Our nanny," he finally said.

"Nellie McGregor?" I clarified.

He nodded. "She came home early with Dolly and Diana from practice one day, and the poor thing walked in on them."

Which explained a lot about her reaction when I'd mentioned her employers to her. "What did she do?"

"She closed the door, walked out and pretended nothing had happened. She didn't say anything for a couple days. But it was right before Valentine's Day, and when I came to her asking what she thought Deb might like, she broke down and told me what she'd seen."

"And what did you do?"

"I confronted Deb. To her credit, she admitted it right away. She said she was sorry, that she'd end it with the guy. But at that point I didn't care. I was too hurt. I told her I needed some time."

"So you separated?"

He nodded. "Yeah."

I shook my head. "But why the floater story? Why make the press think you were the unfaithful one."

"That was Barker's idea." Don squared his jaw, telling me he wasn't entirely thrilled with it even now. "Deb was just about to launch her new book on parenting. Barker knew if something like this came out it would tarnish her image, make the whole book seem like a joke."

"So you were willing to be the joke instead?"

"Look, people will tune in every week to see me being an ass. Boys will be boys, right? I mean, look at Tiger Woods. Hell, some guys even envied him, right? A couple weeks of him looking like a playboy, and he bounces back. But Octomom? She's a villain for life now. No one forgives a mom who makes a mistake."

Sadly, he had a point.

"So Barker suggests this whole ruse, painting you as the bad guy. And you were fine with it?"

"I'm human. Of course I wasn't fine with it."

Ah-ha, now we were getting somewhere. "So why agree?"

"It was the best thing for my kids. You have any idea how expensive it is to raise twelve children? The show is the only way we can make ends meet. And Barker was right about saying the truth would not only ruin Deb's publishing chances, but the show as well. So, I went with his scheme. I figured there were worse things in the world than hanging out with a bunch of co-eds for a few weeks, right?"

"What about Deb? She was fine with this too?"

He shrugged. "She didn't have much of a choice."

"So, the reunion show?" I asked. "Was that Barker's idea, too?"

He nodded. "At first the story of my affair boosted ratings, but after a few weeks it got old. The public moved on. Barker said we need to do something to get back in the headlines for sweeps."

"So he staged a fake reunion?"

Don shrugged. "Look, it wasn't entirely fake. I mean, well, Deb and I are talking. We're seeing a counselor. We've got twelve kids together, you know?"

"Did the kids know what was going on?"

Don shook his head. "All we told them was that Mommy and Daddy needed a little space."

"Hmmm." I wondered if they bought this. While I didn't doubt that Nanny McGregor did her best to shield the children from the media hype, I had a hard time believing the older ones were completely ignorant of what the press said about their family. "What about the other man?" I asked, switching gears. "Who was he?"

Don's jaw squared again. "I don't know. Didn't want to know, to tell you the truth. Look, Deb said it was a mistake. That she'd been seduced. I'm not excusing what she did, and I'm not saying I wasn't hurt. But we were both under a lot of stress. We hardly ever saw each other anymore. It was only a matter of time before something like this was bound to happen."

"It sounds like you don't blame her?"

"Like I said, we're in counseling. I'm hopeful that in time, we'll be able to heal our relationship. She's not a bad person. She just made a bad choice."

A bad choice Barker quickly turned into a media circus. While I was inclined to sympathize with Don's plight, I also realized he had a hell of a reason to want Barker dead. Finding out about his wife's affair then being made to look like the bad guy was like adding insult to a hell of an injury. And, despite Don's cool demeanor now, I wondered if maybe he'd had enough of playing the bad guy.

* * *

I grabbed a drive-thru burger and a Diet Coke before heading back to the *Informer* to type up my notes. As much as I wasn't looking forward to seeing Felix after our argument, I knew I couldn't avoid the place forever. Besides, I had to have something to turn in for tomorrow's edition. Since Don had played the "off the record" card, I figured Lowel's imminent departure from *Stayin' Alive* was the nugget of news to run with. At least, until I found out where Don really was when Barker was killed.

As soon as I got off the elevators I glanced at Felix's office. Luckily he was nowhere to be seen. Tina, however, I noticed was sitting at her desk, hunched over her computer, furiously typing something up.

Hmm, not a good sign. I walked by slowly, trying to read over her shoulder, but no luck. And, even worse, she didn't look up. Whatever story she was typing was that hot.

I walked two cubicles over instead. "Hey Max," I called to its inhabitant.

Max Beacon, the most senior member of the *Informer* staff, wrote the obituary column. I had no idea how old he was, but if I had to guess I'd say he achieved AARP status sometime in the eighties. He kept a bottle of Jim Beam in his top desk drawer, typed all his columns hunt-and-peck style one finger at a time and had his own pre-written obituary, detailing how he died of cirrhosis of the liver, pinned to his cube walls just below a poster of a koala wrapped around a eucalyptus branch asking, "Who needs a hug?" I'd caught Max staring at my boobs more than once since I'd started working here, but as far as I could tell the old guy was harmless.

He turned his watery eyes my way, blinking as they adjusted from the two-dimensional world of his computer screen. "Well, if it isn't my favorite blond bombshell," he said by way of greeting. "What can I do you for?"

"Any idea what Tina's working on?"

He nodded. "Yep."

"Really?" I leaned forward, aware that it showed off a good amount of cleavage. "What is it?"

Max craned his neck, peeking down my shirt. But he shook his head. "Nope."

"Nope?"

"Tina swore me to secrecy. Sorry, kid."

I pouted. "Come on, can't you trust me?"

But he shook his head. "Sorry. She specifically told me not to tell *you*."

"She did, did she?" I leaned back, crossing my arms over my chest to obscure his view.

"Sorry," he said again. Though whether he was sorry he couldn't help me or sorry the peep show was over, I couldn't tell. "Hey, Allie, I gotta ask…" Max leaned in. "Is it true?"

"What?"

"You know, you and the boss…doing the horizontal mambo." Max waggled his generous eyebrows up and down.

"No!"

Max's shoulders sagged. "That's too bad. If the boss was getting laid, he might be in a better mood. I gotta ask for a raise this week, and I could really use him to be in a good mood."

I rolled my eyes. "Sorry my lack of a love life is putting a crimp in your paycheck."

"That's okay," he said, totally ignoring my sarcasm. "I had a feeling it was too good to be true."

I left Max to his sulking and made my way to my own desk. I glanced over the partition toward Tina's cube. Only now it was empty.

I bit my lip. I wasn't sure that was a good sign. Clearly she'd been onto something good. Clearly she'd taken off to follow her hot new lead. Clearly I was in the dark.

Not somewhere I liked being at all.

I stood up, stretched my arms above my head, did a casual glance around the newsroom. No one paid me the slightest attention. I casually sauntered as quickly as I could over to Tina's desk.

Unlike mine, her cube was settled near the back of the newsroom, tucked into a private little corner. I ducked down, figuring I had about five minutes before someone came walking by and noticed me.

I jiggled Tina's mouse, bringing her screen to life. Unfortunately, a window popped up asking for a password. I looked down at her computer keyboard. Due to Felix's squeaky-tight wallet, new equipment was something the *Informer* staff didn't often get to indulge in. The letters on several of the keys on Tina's keyboard were wearing off. I crouched closer, inspecting each key. A few were a bit more worn than others: the "S", "L", "U", and "K".

I took a shot in the dark and typed "skull" into the password slot. I hit the enter button. Unfortunately, it popped me right back to the password screen. No dice. I tried again: "skulls". What do you know? The screen immediately changed, letting me into her system.

I went to her browser history first. Facebook, IMDB, and a criminal records database. All pretty standard, and none that told me anything about her hot lead. I hit most recent documents next, finding a copy of yesterday's column, a love letter to her boyfriend (Tina had a mushy side? Interesting…), an email draft to Cam about a poker night this weekend, and then I hit pay dirt. A copy of the coroner's report on Barker's body. I had no idea how Tina got her hands on it, but I quickly pulled up a browser window and emailed myself a copy. Then I shut Tina's screen off and walked as casually as I could back to my desk.

I sat down and pulled up the report, quickly scanning it. It was pretty much the same info I, and most of Hollywood, already knew. Barker had died of an overdose of Xanax, one of the more common items in Hollywood's medicine cabinets. It was likely administered in a glass of wine. There was a lot of medical mumbo-jumbo detailing the exact location, size and shape of Barker's organs, but if the smoking gun was buried there I had little to no hope of finding it. I scanned the entire report. When I got to the end I read it again, slowly. Clearly something about the report had sparked Tina's interest.

Finally, on the third page, a note at the bottom jumped out at me. It was the coroner's take on Barker's stab wound from the week before his death. It had already begun healing, but there was enough damage left that the coroner detailed the size and shape of the wound. He described it as three inches deep, clean on one side, and made by a serrated blade.

I grabbed a pink Post-it and drew with my sparkly pen the type of weapon that could have made the wound. As I followed the doc's words, a knife materialized on the post-it. Three inches long, two inches thick, with one serrated edge. Could have belonged to any number of knives.

But I felt a shot of adrenalin kick through my system when I realized just what Tina must have. It could have been any number of knives…but it wasn't. The drawing on my post it was an exact replica of the knives that were standard issue to the contestant left in the jungle on *Stayin' Alive*.

Someone on *Stayin' Alive* had stabbed Barker.

Chapter Ten

It had to be Lowel. He'd already confessed to fighting with Barker, he'd threatened him, and he had no alibi for the time of the stabbing. Journalism 101: the most obvious answer is almost always the right one. I felt like such a fool. Lowel had played Gary and me this morning, just like he played millions of viewers every week on TV.

The sheep in wolf's clothing was really a wolf pretending to be a sheep pretending to be a wolf.

I grabbed my purse, hit the stairs running and jumped behind the wheel of my Bug. I'd gunned the engine and was peeling out of the lot with a screech to my tires when I realized I had no idea where I was going. Lowel's commercial shoot had ended hours ago. And I had no clue where he was staying in town. I pulled over to the side of the road and dialed Cam's number on my cell.

Three rings into it, she picked up. "Cameron Dakota?"

"Hey, it's Allie. Remember how Tina sent you over to spy on me, and how bad you felt that you actually almost did?"

There was a pause, then, "Um…yeah?"

"It's time to make up for that. I need a favor."

"What kind of favor?"

"I need to know where Lowel Simonson is staying while he's in town."

"Hang on," Cam said, and I could hear the sound of her keyboard clacking. "Okay, the last photos I have of him are coming out of the Beverly Wilshire last night. I'd say that's your best bet."

"Presidential suite?" I asked.

"Knowing Lowel, that would be my guess."

"Thanks!" I shouted before hanging up and quickly merging back into traffic again.

Which, unfortunately, at this time of day was thick. I looked down at my watch. Four-fifteen. The roads were clogged like overburdened arteries to every limb of the city, every possible route to the mid-Wilshire area blocked by a sea of other commuters all trying to beat the traffic.

I jiggled my knee at a red light, twisted a lock of hair at a stop sign, came up with a whole string of creative curses when I got stuck behind a stalled car in the left lane on Le Brea. I was about to jump out of my skin by the time I finally found a parking spot on the street across from the Beverly Wilshire hotel. I quickly got out, fed the meter and locked my car.

At exactly the same time that I saw Tina's motorcycle screech to a halt in the alleyway beside the hotel. She pulled her helmet off and looked up. We locked eyes. We both froze for a half a second before springing into action, each of us racing for the front doors of the BW.

She hit the doors first but I was a quick step behind, entering the lobby just as she dove into an elevator and pressed the doors closed behind her. I dashed for the stairs, taking them two at a time. All those hours on the stepper came in handy as I jammed up the eight flights, hitting the hallway just as the doors of the elevator opened. Tina dashed out, making a beeline for Presidential's front door. I did the same, my breath coming hard as I came in from the left.

We hit the doors at the same time, half knocking on them, half body-slamming them.

"What are you doing here?" Tina hissed.

"Following a lead," I shot back, wheezing between my words.

"You mean, following *my* lead.'

I blinked innocently at her. "I can't imagine what you mean by that."

"Look, Felix may buy that adorable blond act you've got going on, but I know you're a lying, cheating little—"

Luckily she didn't get to finish. The door opened in front of us. Lowel Simonson, swathed in a silk bathrobe, stared at the two of us on his doorstep. "May I help you?" he asked, his gaze going from Tina to me.

Tina didn't miss a beat, quickly sticking one hand out toward Lowel. "Hi. Tina Bender."

He stared at it then up at me. "Is she with your Japanese paper too?"

Tina frowned, opened her mouth to speak then apparently thought better of it as she closed it and turned to me instead, letting me field that one.

I nodded. "Yes. We had just a few follow-up questions we'd like to ask you," I said. Which was true enough, even if our journalistic affiliation was a little fudged.

Lowel nodded. "Fine. But let's make this quick. I have a massage in ten minutes."

He stepped back allowing Tina and I entry.

"Japanese paper?" she whispered out of the corner of her mouth.

"Go with it," I urged.

While there was nothing in this world I wanted to do less than share an interview with Tina, it was clear this was the only way I was going to get to Lowel today. Better to question him in tandem than not at all.

We followed him into a sitting area twice the size of my entire apartment. A baby grand piano sat by the windows, with two immaculate white lounge chairs, a chaise and a full-sized sofa filling out the room.

"Please, sit down," the wolf-slash-sheep-slash-wolf said, gesturing to the sofa as he sank down onto the chaise.

"Thank you." I only hoped he'd be as cordial once we hit him with our damning evidence.

"So, what can I help you with?" Lowel asked.

I opened my mouth to tell him, but Tina pounced first. "Where is your knife?"

Lowel's eyebrows jumped north, but the rest of his features remained impassive, a testament to his plastic surgeon's skills. "I beg your pardon. Knife?"

"Every contestant on *Stayin' Alive* is outfitted with a survival knife at the beginning of the show."

"And I have never been a contestant," he pointed out.

"True," Tina conceded. "But at the end of season seven, Rebecca Lamm from Freeport, Illinois was so overcome at winning the competition after beating the favorite, Chicago Phil, in both the kayaking challenge and the Spanish Tango that she presented her knife to you as a token of appreciation for your constructive criticism on her dance moves."

I had to admit I was impressed. Clearly Tina watched a lot more trash TV than I did.

And a lot more than Lowel had counted on as well. He

shifted uncomfortably in his seat. "I suppose she did."

"So, where is that knife now?"

"I…I don't know."

"I have a theory!" I piped up.

Tina shot me a look, but I ignored her, plowing ahead. "And correct me if I'm wrong, Lowel," I said, turning to our host. "But I think your knife is somewhere on the Sunset Studios lot. Wanna know why I think that?"

Lowel shifted again. Clearly he did not.

"Oh, I'd love to know why," Tina said, playing right along now in my game of good cop, bad cop.

"I think it's still on the lot because that's where Lowel tossed it after he stabbed Chester Barker in the back with it."

"That's a lie!" Lowel shouted, springing up from his chair so quickly his robe flapped open. I quickly looked away. There were some parts a plastic surgeon wouldn't touch, and I so did not want to know how saggy those were.

"I don't think it's a lie," I countered. "I think you were more upset with Barker than you let on. Friends or not, he was firing you, replacing you with a younger model."

I saw Tina raise an eyebrow beside me and did a mental fist-pump—I knew something about Lowel she didn't.

"You were like the first wife who spent her best years making him a success, just to be tossed aside for a hot young tart," I added.

Tina shot me a look that clearly questioned whether I had any experience as said "tart" but I brushed it aside, focusing on Lowel.

"Just a guess here, but I'm thinking you enjoy your first-wife status, Lowel," I continued. "I mean, out-of-work reality show hosts can't usually afford massages in the Presidential suite, can they?"

Lowel turned red, tugged his robe tighter to his body.

"So, you did the only thing you could do, didn't you? You stabbed Barker to save your career."

"You have no proof!" he sputtered.

"We have the coroner's report," Tina jumped in.

I nodded. "That's right. It's very interesting reading. Have you looked at it, Lowel?"

He didn't answer, but his artfully tanned skin seemed to pale a shade.

"It details," I went on, "the exact size and shape of Barker's stab wound. Which, incidentally, is one-hundred percent consistent with the unique *Stayin' Alive* knives."

Tina nodded in agreement. "Completely consistent."

Lowel's Adam's apple bobbed up and down. "Dozens of people had that same knife. You know how many of those we've given out throughout the seasons?"

"A lot," I nodded in agreement.

"One hundred and eight, to be exact," Tina chimed in. Dang, the girl did her homework. "But guess how many of those one hundred and eight people were on the guest list at the party where Barker was stabbed."

Lowel clenched his jaw. He clearly wasn't in the mood for a guessing game.

"I have a guess!" I said, raising my hand.

Tina nodded at me. "Allie?"

"Zero?"

"Correct. Big, fat zero."

She stared at Lowel. I stared at Lowel.

Lowel seemed to shrink inside his robe, finally sinking back down onto the chaise. "All right, fine," he sighed, his shoulders sagging. "You're right. I stabbed Barker. Happy?"

To be honest, I was a little.

"What happened?" Tina asked, leaning in.

"It was all like you said. *Stayin' Alive* made Barker, and I made *Stayin' Alive*. That man wouldn't even have a career if it weren't for me! And how did he thank me? By firing me. Nine years I'd given that creep, and he dumps me like I'm Charlie Sheen."

"So, you stabbed him," Tina said.

Lowel nodded. To his credit, he looked sheepish and guilty as hell. "I wasn't thinking. I was angry. It was a spur-of-the-moment thing. He was standing with a couple other producers, telling them all how he was getting rid of dead weight on his shows this season. I knew he was talking about me. The way he was laughing, preening, so pleased with himself. I just snapped."

"And you stabbed him."

Lowel nodded again. "I never meant to really hurt him. You have no idea how relieved I was when the hospital said he was going to be fine."

"Relieved enough to poison him two weeks later?" Tina suggested.

"What? No!" Lowel shook his head violently from left to right. "Look, I stabbed Barker out of blind rage, but I didn't kill him!"

"And why should we believe you now?" I asked.

"Because it's the truth!"

"Prove it," Tina challenged. "Give us an alibi. Where were you the night he was killed?

Lowel looked from me to Tina then back again. He clamped his thin lips shut and shook his head. "I'm sorry, I can't tell you that."

"Because you were busy poisoning Barker that night?" she asked.

"No!"

"Then where were you?"

He sat back in his seat, crossing his arms over his chest.

"Fine." I shrugged. "You don't want to tell us? You can just tell the police when we let them know it was you who stabbed Barker."

"You can't prove that," Lowel tried again. "It's my word against yours."

I watched as Tina grinned. A horrible, wonderful, evil grin. Usually I was the recipient of that look, but this time it was all focused on Lowel. "*Au contraire*, my friend." She reached into her purse and pulled out a micro recorder. "It's your word against yours. I just got it all on tape."

That was twice in one day Tina's skills had impressed me. If I didn't watch out, I was liable to start admiring her or something.

Lowel, on the other hand, blanched. Then his shoulders slumped and, despite the work of his excellent plastic surgeon, his face sagged, looking suddenly all of his nearly fifty-one years.

"Fine. Look, I'll tell you where I was. But this cannot be printed. Ever. It's strictly off the record."

"Fine," Tina and I said in unison. Though I'm pretty sure I saw Tina's fingers cross behind her back.

"I was with Sergio Melendez."

I wrote down the name. "Where?"

Lowel squirmed in his seat. "At his studio. His dance studio."

I wrote it down. "Okay. And?" I asked, waiting for the punch line.

"And I was at his studio taking dance lessons."

I blinked at the man.

"It's true," he said, his eyes tearing up as he explained. "I'm a sham! I don't know how to dance to save my life. I have the worst rhythm of anyone you've ever seen. Four left feet, to tell the truth. It's all fake."

Mental forehead smack. "You're serious?"

Lowel hung his head. "I'm afraid so."

I thought I heard Tina snort beside me.

"So all that yelling at the contestants on the show about their poor technique?"

"Totally talking out my ass," Lowel whined. "I never even saw a tango until the finale of season one."

"And Barker knew this?" I couldn't help asking.

Lowel nodded. "Didn't care. Said I had the presence he was looking for. Barker was a showman."

So I was beginning to see. I made a mental note to ask Alec how much he knew about it.

"I assume Sergio can confirm your alibi?" Tina asked.

Lowel nodded. "Yes, he'll tell you I was there. Go ahead and ask him. Discreetly, of course," he added.

"Of course."

* * *

As soon as we stepped outside the doors to Lowel's suite, Tina whipped out her cell and began texting like mad. I peered over her shoulder as we waited for the elevator, but she covered her screen with her thumbs and shot me a dirty look.

"If you want to know what I'm doing, you can ask instead of snooping," she said.

I rolled my eyes. "Fine. Tina, may I ask who you're texting?"

"Yes, you may. I'm checking on Lowel's alibi. I happen to know an up-and-coming actress who also takes lessons with Sergio. I'm asking her to ask him about the night Barker died."

"Is there anyone in Hollywood you don't know?" I asked. Only slightly sarcastically.

Tina paused a moment. Then shook her head. "Within a Kevin-Bacon degree? No."

I hated her.

The elevator arrived and by the time we hit the lobby doors, Tina's phone was beeping with return texts.

"Confirmed," she said, a distinct note of disappointment coloring her voice. "Lowel was with Sergio from ten to midnight."

"Your informant is sure?"

Tina nodded. "Totally. Sergio said he was sore for days afterward. Apparently Lowel stepped on his feet. Numerous times."

"Great. So we're back to square one."

Tina sent me a sidelong glance. "Well, maybe *you* are. I have a few viable leads still."

I narrowed my eyes at her, trying to decide if she was bluffing or not. "By the way," I said. "I'd appreciate it if you'd stop telling everyone I'm sleeping with Felix."

She blinked innocently at me. "Whatever do you mean?"

"I mean, stay out of my business."

"You mean, like you stayed out of mine by stealing my story?"

"I didn't steal anything. Felix gave it to me."

"Right. Because you are Felix's—"

I shot her a death look.

"—favorite," she finished. Though I had the distinct feeling that hadn't been her first word choice.

"Can I help it if I deliver?" I retorted.

"Look, you follow your leads, and I'll follow mine," Tina shot back. "We'll see who delivers this story first."

"Fine."

"Fine!"

"Fine!"

We both stared at each other a beat. Then Tina turned on her black boots and marched to her motorcycle, revving the engine as she shoved a helmet on her head.

Because I was ninety-nine percent sure she was zooming to the *Informer* to turn in a story with her name front and solo on it, I quickly jumped in my Bug and pulled up my dictation program to run while I navigated traffic back to the offices.

Not surprisingly, her Honda was a little bit better at navigating between the stalled traffic, and she beat me there. I was just pulling into a spot near the back of the lot when my cell rang.

"What!" I barked, grabbing my bag, laptop, notes.

"Whoa. You always answer the phone that way?" came Felix's voice.

I bit my lip. "Sorry," I said, taking my volume down several notches.

"Yes, well, so am I."

I paused. I glanced up at the second floor windows. Was Felix actually calling to apologize? Granted, he'd been totally in the wrong to tell me that my biggest assets to the paper were my tits, but I was impressed to hear he was big enough to admit it. "You are?" I asked.

"Yes."

What do you know? He *was* apologizing.

"Sorry," he added, "that I don't have your copy yet."

And just like that, he had to ruin it.

"Right. Because copy is all you care about." I slammed my car door shut, heading for the elevator.

"I'm sorry, do I detect a smidgeon of attitude?" he asked.

"Who me? Nope. I'm perky, happy sunshine."

"That was more than a smidgeon." He paused. "Do I want to know?"

I stepped off the elevator doors on the second floor. I could see him pacing in his glass office, one hand to his Bluetooth.

"If you don't know, then I'm certainly not telling you," I countered.

"Then why are we even having this discussion?"

"We're not!"

"Wonderful. Your copy?" he pressed.

I pushed through the doors to his office. "Just sent it. Check your inbox."

He spun around, clearly surprised to see me. "Oh. Hi," he said, hanging up.

I kept my mouth shut, giving him a mini silent treatment. But he didn't seem to notice, instead moving to his computer screen, pulling up his inbox, and scanning my story.

"You've been busy today."

"Yes. My *assets* have gotten a full workout."

He raised an eyebrow at me but before he could come up with some bitingly British remark, I continued, "Now, if you'll excuse me, I have somewhere to be."

"Hot lead?" Felix asked.

I put my hands on my hips. "As a matter of fact, yes."

He paused. Raised his eyes to meet mine. Lifted his eyebrows ever so slightly. "Who?"

"Alec Davies. I'm meeting him for dinner."

Felix stared at me for a beat, some indefinable emotion flitting behind his eyes. "Dinner?"

"Yes."

"That sounds personal."

I paused. "He's got footage of Don and Deb for me to look at."

"He could drop that off here."

"He could," I agreed.

"So, why the dinner?"

I squared my shoulders. "Okay, so maybe this is a little personal. I am allowed to have a personal life, aren't I?"

Felix gave me a long, hard stare. "No."

I blinked. "What do you mean, 'no?'"

"No, you're not allowed to have a personal life where Alec Davies is concerned."

"Oh, yes I am," I said, my volume rising.

"No, you're not."

"Yes. I. Am."

"No. You're. Not."

I narrowed my eyes. "Excuse me, but you have no right whatsoever to tell me what to do."

"I'm your boss."

"You're not the boss of my love life."

He paused. "Love? Just how personal has this gotten already?"

I squared my shoulders, making the most of my meager height. "That is none of your business," I replied. Even though, quite frankly, there wasn't much to tell. But even if there was, no way was I telling Felix.

"I want you off this," Felix said, turning to his computer. "I'm giving Davies to Tina."

"Like hell you are!" I shouted. "You're the one who told me I should use my assets. Well, that's what I'm doing. You don't like the outcome, that's your fault."

Felix took a step toward me. "You are not to go near Davies again, you hear me?"

"Why? Because he's cute? Successful? Into me?"

Felix took another step toward me, pinning me to the spot with a look so intent I had to stop myself from physically backing away. "No, Allie," he responded, his voice hard and commanding, "because Davies is a convicted felon."

Chapter Eleven

I'll admit it, that nugget of information stunned the snide remarks right out of me. "What?" I breathed out once I'd found my voice again. "What do you mean, 'felon?'"

"I mean, he's been convicted of a felony."

"You must be mistaken."

Felix shook his head. "I assure you, I'm not."

"Where did you get this information?"

"From Tina. And she's never mistaken."

I thought a really bad word directed at one purple-haired reporter.

"Where did she get it?" I asked. Even though the second the words left my mouth, I remembered the criminal database I'd seen in her browser history earlier. Apparently she hadn't been bluffing at the hotel when she'd alluded to an ace up her sleeve.

Felix crossed the room to his computer and jiggled the mouse to life. A few clicks later, a picture of a younger-looking Alec filled his screen. In a mug shot.

"I don't believe it," I whispered, taking in the photo.

Only, of course, the proof was here staring me in the face. And I felt like a fool. I'd let his dimples and easy smile distract me from good investigating. I was better than that.

"What was he convicted of?" I asked, hoping Felix said jaywalking.

"Theft."

Damn.

"Apparently," Felix went on, "grand theft auto, according to his rap sheet."

"He stole a car?"

"Fifteen cars."

Yikes. "So, why isn't he in jail now?"

"He was a juvenile at the time," Felix said, reading off the screen where a detailed rap sheet accompanied the unflattering photo, "and was living in Canada then. He served a couple years in prison there, then was let out when he turned twenty-one."

I stared at the picture again. He'd been just a kid. He hardly looked like a hardened criminal. Then again, he'd had time to harden up since. And what better place to do so than in prison.

"I don't know. I still have a hard time picturing him as Barker's killer," I hedged.

"Does he have an alibi?" Felix asked.

"Um…"

"You did ask him for an alibi, didn't you?" He narrowed his eyes at me.

"Sorta. I mean, I kinda got distracted."

"Hmm." His eyes narrowed even further, reminding me of a cat ready to pounce. "But he was the last person to see Barker alive?"

"I guess."

"And, as Barker's partner, he does now have sole control over the company."

"I hadn't thought of that."

"Had you thought to ask him if he and Barker were on good terms?"

"Okay, fine!" I said, throwing my hands up in the air. "I dropped the ball on this one, okay? Happy?"

"I'm not sure why my reporter dropping the ball should make me happy."

"Look, this is all the more reason why I should see Alec tonight. I need to get the straight story out of him."

"No." Felix shook his head. "No way am I letting you put yourself in harm's way like this."

"He's not very well going to kill me in the middle of Mangia."

Felix's eyebrows shot up. "He got reservations at Mangia?"

I nodded.

He shook his head. "Wow. They told me they had a six-week wait."

"It pays to be a producer."

"It doesn't matter," he said, shaking his head. "I can't let you go out with this guy. It's not worth the risk."

"Might I point out it isn't your place to 'let' or 'not let' me do anything?"

"I said no. End of discussion."

"You can't tell me what to do. I'm not a child."

"Then quit acting so damned childish!" he shouted.

"Me?" I shouted back. Loudly enough that Max's head popped up over the top of his partition to see what the commotion was about. "I'm not the one letting my petty jealousy get in the way of good reporting."

"Ha!" Felix barked, though there was zero humor in the sound. "Jealousy? You think I'm jealous of some two-bit felon turned wannabe producer?"

"He's pulling seven figures a year. He's hardly a wannabe."

"Allie, love, if you think this is personal…" Felix trailed off and shook his head. Then he lowered his voice and sent me a look that smacked of pity. "Look, Allie, it was just one night."

I clenched my jaw shut, my cheeks instantly filling with the heat of an embarrassing one-nighter, turned into an even more embarrassing encounter with a boss who thought I was harboring some childish crush I clearly was not. I squared my shoulders, mustering up as much dignity as I could. "I'm sorry, I have to go. I have a date."

Then, for the second day in a row, I stormed out of his office (though, this time I'm happy to say I remembered to grab my purse first) and stomped across the floor as noisily as my heels could muster.

* * *

I drove home, took a hot shower and defiantly painted my toenails a hot passion pink. Only, I had to admit that even after I calmed down, the whole felon thing stuck with me. While I had a hard time picturing Alec's adorable dimples killing anyone, I figured it was better to be safe than sorry. So while I waited for my toenails to dry I dialed Gary's number

I waited while the phone rang three times on the other end, then a sleepy voice picked up.

"What?"

"Hey, Gary, it's Allie."

"Allie who?'

"Quick."

There was a pause.

"The reporter?" I pressed.

"Oh, right," he said stifling a yawn.

"Listen, I need you to help me out tonight."

I could feel him slowly coming awake on the other end. "Uhn uh. No way, blondie. Last time I helped you, I nearly got run off the road. I've got a welt on the head so nasty I've been sleeping all afternoon."

"Sleeping. The favorite pastime of the *unemployed*," I reminded him.

He paused. "You offering me a real job?"

"If you help me out tonight, you're hired as my assistant."

"Do I get benefits?"

"You're pushing it."

"Okay, fine. What do you want me to do?"

"I'm interviewing a suspect tonight. I want you to follow us and just keep close in case I need backup."

"What kind of backup?"

I quickly filled him in on Alec's record and my sudden wariness at being alone with him tonight.

"So, I'm like your bodyguard," Gary said when I was done.

"Backup," I corrected.

"Right. I'm on it. The second I see trouble, I'll be ready to kick some ass."

"No! No ass kicking. I just need you to keep an eye out. If there's trouble, call nine-one-one."

"Fine. I'll call nine-one-one," he sighed. Then added, "You're no fun."

That was the least of my worries.

* * *

Once I had my backup settled, I blow-dried and styled my hair, doing the big, soft curls thing with just the slightest hint of styling wax that left my hair looking naturally soft and touchable, yet totally frizz-free. Then I went full force on the smoky eyes, lots of thick black liner, black lengthening mascara, and gray eyeshadow with just the slightest hint of purple along the edges to bring out my green eyes. After a thick swipe of pale pink lipstick, I was looking pretty hot, even if I did say so myself.

Careful not to smudge the mascara, I slid a short, silver tank

dress over my head. It was a simple cut, ending just enough
inches above my knee to turn heads, but not enough to say I was
available by the hour. A V-neck gave the illusion of elongating
my stature, and the low drop in the back said sexy in a very
classy way. I finished off the outfit with a pair of black three-
inch strappy stilettos, leaving myself just enough time to be only
slightly fashionably late to the restaurant.

Which, as it turned out, was every bit as amazing as a six-
week wait would have you imagine. As I parked across the
street, for a moment I forgot I was a reporter peeking into the
lives of the rich and famous; I actually felt as if I was one of the
elite.

I saw two paparazzi outside, flashing their cameras in the
faces of anyone semi-recognizable as they left. Just for kicks I
ducked my head, pretending to be someone famous enough not
to want to be photographed. I couldn't help a little giggle as I
saw a flash go off to my right.

"Hey, sweetie," the guy behind the camera called. "What's
your name?"

I flipped my hair over my right shoulder. "Allie Quick.
Newest star reporter for the *L.A. Times*." Hey, if I was
fantasizing I might as well go all the way, right?

Out of the corner of my eye I saw the guy pull out this cell,
no doubt Tweeting this tidbit as I slipped through the door. Gotta
love a desperate paparazzo.

The interior of the restaurant was just as swanky as the
outside. Red velvet walls, crystal chandeliers and gilded frames
glittering with a luxury that was just this side of opulence. As I
took in the décor I heard my cell chirp to life in my pocketbook.
I pulled it out. Felix's number.

I resisted giving a very unladylike snort. Nice try, mister,
but I was going Felix-free tonight. I put the phone on silent mode
before shoving it back into my purse. Then I gave my name to
the maitre d', and he quickly whisked me to a table near the
center of the room where Alec was waiting, a bottle of
champagne chilling in a gold bucket to his right.

Maybe it was just me, but he was looking decidedly un-
murderer-like. He was dressed in a dark blazer, casually layered
over a blue button-down shirt opened at the neck. A pair of jeans

beneath said he was too cool to worry about dressing up, but his Armani loafers showed he knew how to dress when the occasion called for it. He stood when I approached the table, his dimples appearing as he did a slow smile. Suddenly I felt foolish for ever worrying about my safety. No one this good-looking could be guilty, right?

"That's quite a dress," he said, his eyes flickering to my hemline.

"I'm quite a gal."

He grinned. "I believe it," he laughed as he pulled my chair out for me.

As I sat, I sent a casual glance toward the bar area. Gary had taken up residence on a stool next to a tall redhead in a blue miniskirt. He raised a martini glass my way and gave me an exaggerated wink before turning his attention back to the redhead.

"So, what are you in the mood for tonight?" Alec said.

I quickly shifted my gaze to him from my would-be bodyguard as Alec handed me a menu.

It was half in Italian, all the prices withheld. I figured it was the kind of place where if you had to ask, you couldn't afford it. I chalked it up to my guilt at having been rehearsing my interrogation tactics the entire way here down the 405 that I picked out the least expensive-sounding item, going with the porcini mushroom fettuccini in white wine sauce. Alec ordered the steak, medium rare. In perfect Italian.

I downed my champagne in one gulp, forcing myself to ignore the sexy lilt of the language rolling off his tongue and remember why I was really here. "Alec, I have to ask you something," I said, setting my elegant glass down.

Immediately a waiter appeared at my elbow, filling it to the top again. Which was fine with me. I figured I needed all the liquid courage I could get tonight.

"Uh, it's about the Barker story," I continued.

"Right," Alec said. Then before I could continue, he reached into the inner pocket of his blazer, coming out with a slim, black memory stick. He pushed it across the table to me.

"The footage you wanted of Don and Deb. This is everything we shot the day Barker died. I'm not sure if any of it

will be helpful—it was mostly of the kids—but it's all yours."
He shot me that blinding smile again and winked.

I felt myself blush and cleared my throat. Took another sip
(okay, it was more like a generous swig) of champagne.
"Thanks. For this," I added, slipping the memory stick into my
purse. "But, actually, that's not what I wanted talk to you about."

"Oh?" he asked, refilling my glass (that had somehow
become empty again). "Okay, what is it then? Shoot," he
encouraged, giving me a smile that reached all the way to his
eyes, crinkling in a quite lovely way at the corners.

I bit my lip, really wishing I didn't have to. "It's about
Canada," I hedged.

"I can tell you anything *a-boot* Canada that you want to
know," he joked, emphasizing the northern pronunciation.

I couldn't help a smile. Though it was short-lived as I dove
in. "What can you tell me about Canadian prisons?"

His grin faltered. "Excuse me?"

I let out a deep breath, leaning in close. "Look, I found out
about your felony conviction."

He stared at me for a second then leaned back in his chair,
the grin a distant memory. He steepled his fingers together,
assessing me in silence for a moment.

I felt myself fidget under his gaze even though he was the
one with the record.

Finally he said, "Okay. Yes. I've spent time in jail."

I felt relief drain out of me that he didn't try to deny it.
"Why didn't you tell me?"

"It's not something I'm exactly proud of. I don't usually
lead with it when I'm trying to impress a girl."

I bit my lip. He wanted to impress me. Man, it was hard to
interrogate a pair of dimples that wanted to impress you.

"So, you admit you stole cars?" I forced myself to press on.

He lean forward again, this time putting his elbow on the
table and lowering his voice to an intimate tone. "I was young.
Not that I'm making excuses. It was a stupid thing to do. Idiotic.
But my cousin, Jack, had this chop shop. I was sixteen, and my
family wasn't exactly what you'd call well off. I had two
choices—I could get a job flipping burgers for minimum wage,
or I could go work for Jack. I chose Jack. It was clearly the

wrong choice, and I paid for it."

I licked my lips. "How long were you in jail?"

"Three years."

"Must have been tough."

I could tell by the look in his eyes it was. Even just talking about it now, his jaw was stiff, his gaze guarded, his entire posture changed from the open, laid-back producer to a cornered criminal used to watching his back.

But instead of agreeing with me, he shrugged. "I deserved every day I spent there. But I can tell you, as soon as I got out I left that life behind me. I got a work visa, moved to L.A. and right away got a job with Barker."

"So, that was what you meant when you said he gave you a chance."

He nodded. "Barker knew about my past. Hell, there wasn't any way I could have hid it from him. It's on my official record. But he saw something in me. A willingness to work hard, to start at the bottom. I had a lot to make up for after I got out, and he gave me an opportunity to do that."

"I'm sorry," I said.

He raised an eyebrow at me. "For?"

"For your loss. It sounds like Barker was more than just a co-worker."

Alec smiled slowly. "Yeah, he was. And thanks."

He sat up straight, shaking the moment off, and grabbed the champagne bottle, refilling both our glasses. "So, now you know my sordid past," he said, flashing a dimple my way, "my turn to learn about yours."

I grinned in response. "Fair enough. Just promise me one thing: no more secrets, okay?"

He nodded and flashed me a smile that could charm the panties off a nun. "I'll drink to that."

* * *

I sipped at about three more glasses (and ignored my phone buzzing silently in my purse half a dozen more times) as I told Alec about my job at the *Informer*, my real aspirations of being a *Times* reporter, about Tina, and even about my penny-pinching, over-bearing, annoyingly British boss. By the time Alec finally paid the bill, I'd spilled pretty much my entire life story and I think at least ten dollars worth of champagne (somehow those glasses got harder to hold onto as the evening wore on).

Alec put a hand at the small of my back as he led me through the restaurant, back out into the warm night air. Which was a good thing, because for some reason as we exited the restaurant, my stilettos seemed to have grown wobbly. As we stepped out onto the sidewalk one of the paparazzi snapped a photo, his flash momentarily blinding me as my shoe collapsed under my foot.

"Whoa," Alec said. His arms went around my waist, holding me up.

I giggled. I mean, I think it was me, but it sounded more like Miley Cyrus than a grown woman.

"You okay?" he asked. He was grinning down at me, his smile close enough that I felt his breath on my cheek.

Was I ever. I nodded. Then unconsciously licked my lips.

His eyes followed the motion of my tongue, glazing over, going just that much darker.

"Sorry. I guess I'm not used to champagne," I said.

"Maybe we ought to get you home," he mumbled, his voice low. Intimate. Infused with meaning.

I licked my lips again, nodding in what I hoped wasn't an overly eager way.

He leaned down, and I watched in slow motion as his warm, full mouth moved toward mine. I close my eyes, lifted my chin, prepared to feel the softness of his kiss...

And instead felt him being ripped from my arms with a loud, "Oof."

I opened my eyes. Alec was on the ground, spread eagle, a four-foot tall person on top of him pounding him with pudgy fists.

"I got him!" Gary yelled. "Don't worry! I got him."

I rolled my eyes. "Jesus, Gary, what are you doing? Get off of him!"

Though I noticed that Alec had already managed to extricate himself from Gary's rain of little fists.

"What the hell are you doing?" I yelled as my *back-up*

stood up, brushing himself off.

He blinked at me. "What do you mean, what am I doing? I'm rescuing you."

Oh, brother.

"Do I look like I need rescuing?"

"He was attacking you!"

"He was kissing me!"

Gary looked from me to Alec. "Well, from the back it looked a lot like attacking."

I threw my hands up.

"A friend of yours?" Alec asked, brushing off his blazer.

"Alec, meet Gary."

"I'm her bodyguard."

Alec raised an eyebrow at me.

"*Assistant*," I clarified. "Who is leaving, unless he wants to find himself suddenly unemployed again."

Gary put his hands up in a surrender motion. "Okay, okay. Geez. I was just doing my job…" He trailed off as he ducked back into the restaurant, presumably back to his redhead. Though I didn't really care where Gary went. What I was more focused on was Alec.

And the sudden two feet of distance between us.

I cleared my throat. "Um, sorry about that."

Alec grinned, though it was a shallow thing. Clearly being pummeled on the sidewalk wasn't high on his list of aphrodisiacs. "Right. No problem. Happens all the time," he joked.

"Yeah." I cleared my throat, shifted from my left foot to my right. "So, um…"

"I had a really nice evening," Alec jumped in.

"Right. Me too."

"No, I mean it," he said. And he took a step closer, closing some of the gap. "Really nice."

I couldn't help smiling back. "Me too."

"Can I walk you to your car?"

I shook my head. "No, I'm good. I think I'm actually gonna take a cab."

"I could give you a ride?" he offered. But I could tell the intimate insinuations of a moment earlier were gone from the offer.

I shook my head. "I'm good. Really. But thanks."

"Anytime," he responded. "Well, have a good night. And we'll talk soon, yes?"

I nodded. "Definitely."

He leaned in and gave me a quick peck on the cheek before walking toward the parking garage down the street.

Not exactly the way I'd hoped to end the evening just a few minutes ago, but considering the circumstances I figured it wasn't the worst way the evening could end, either.

* * *

It was after midnight before my cab pulled up in front of my building in Glendale. I got as far as my front door before my cell buzzed to life in my purse for the umpteenth time. I pulled it out, checking the readout. Felix. Again.

I stabbed my finger at the On button. "What do you want?" I barked out.

"Jesus, don't you ever pick up your phone?"

"I'm picking up now."

"I've called ten times."

"I know," I gritted out between clenched teeth. "I was busy."

"On your date."

"Yes. As you well know," I couldn't help pointing out.

"And?"

"And what?"

"Details."

"I am not giving you details about my love life," I said, shoving the key in my front door.

There was a pause on the other end. Then, "I meant details about the interview."

"Oh."

"Look, Allie," he said.

But whatever followed was lost in a blur as I entered my front door, switched on the lights, and got a look at my place.

My sofa had been de-slipcovered, the cushions slit open until their stuffing innards spewed out onto the floor. My vase of daisies had been shattered, flowers and water strewn across the coffee table. Every cupboard in my kitchen was open, the contents spilled out in a haphazard fashion that said this was more for show than an intent to find valuables.

I took a couple of tentative steps into the room, feeling my feet crunch on cereal and glass shards. My mouth hung open as I surveyed the chaos that used to be my pretty little sanctuary.

Someone had totally trashed the place.

"Mr. Fluffykins?" I squeaked out. I cleared my throat then tried again. "Mr. Fluffykins? Are you okay?"

"What?" I heard Felix ask in my ear. "Who's Mr. Fluffykins? Are you even listening to me?"

"Mr. Fluffykins!" I called out again, hearing the fear lacing my own voice, listening for a telltale mewing in response.

Nothing.

I felt tears back up behind my eyes.

"Who is Mr. Fluffykins?" Felix repeated.

"My Cat. Oh God, what did they do to my cat? Mr. Fluffykins!" I shouted this time, springing into action. I peered under the sofa, behind the open cupboards, in the scant three inches between the refrigerator and the counter.

"'They?' Who is 'they'? What's going on over there?" I heard Felix ask.

But I was too focused to answer. To say I was frantic would be a gross understatement. Tears ran down my face, my hands shaking, my brain going over the last time I'd fed him and how I was such a cruel owner that his last meal might have been dry cat mix instead of premium Chicken of the Sea tuna.

"Mr. Fluffykins! Where are you? Mommy's sorry! Please be okay! Please come out, Mr. Fluffykins."

"Allie—"

"Shh!" I commanded. I froze. I thought I heard a noise. A very faint sound coming from the bathroom.

I dashed across the room and threw open the bathroom door, barely registering the mess inside as a fluffy ball of fur slunk out from behind the toilet.

"Ohmigod, Mr. Fluffykins!" I sank to my knees, hugging the cat to my chest, completely ignoring the claws digging into my arm. "Oh, Mr. Fluffykins, I'm so glad you're okay! I'm so sorry I left you alone. I'm sorry I didn't feed you tuna. I'm sorry—"

But that's as far as I got. Because as I hugged my scared cat to my chest, I heard a noise behind me.

I spun around...

Too late. A loud crack reverberated through my head. I only had a split second to register pain exploding behind my right ear before the entire world went black.

Chapter Twelve

"Allie? Allie, are you okay? Speak to me, Allie."

I heard Felix's voice from very far away. Was he still on the phone? I tried to move my mouth to speak but only got as far as twitching my lips before I realized that hurt. A lot. I groaned.

"Allie?" Felix asked again. "Wake up."

I didn't wanna. Waking up sounded painful. Everything felt painful, each breath I took hammering in my head.

"Allie?"

But since it was clear Felix wasn't giving up, I slowly tried to open my eyes. It felt as if the lids had been glued shut, and it now took an act of superhuman strength to lift them even an inch. I blinked once. Twice.

"Allie. I'm here."

And I realized, as my eyes started to focus on the room, that he was. Felix wasn't just on the phone, he was sitting on the cracked tile floor of my bathroom, holding my head in his hands, his sandy brows drawn into a tight, concerned line as he stared down at me. "Say something," he commanded.

I swallowed. "Something," I croaked out.

Relief washed over his features. "Christ, don't you ever do that to me again."

"To you? I'm the one on the bathroom floor," I pointed out.

"Can you move?" he asked, concern marring his features again.

"I don't wanna."

"Try."

Boy, he wasn't gonna give up, was he?

I wiggled my fingers, toes, moved one leg. So far, so good. Nothing seemed to be broken, disconnected or otherwise harmed. Except the goose egg I could feel brewing on the side of my head.

I tried to haul myself to a sitting position, feeling my butt go numb on the cold tiles. The room wobbled in my vision as I went vertical, but after blinking hard a few times it stood still, and my stomach stopped threatening to seize up on me.

"You okay?" Felix asked.

I nodded. Bad idea. More spinning. "Where's my cat?" I croaked out.

"I closed him up in the bedroom. He kept hissing at me."

Good Mr. Fluffykins.

I slowly stretched my limbs, moving to a full standing position, holding onto my pedestal sink for support as I took stock of my surroundings.

Lipstick had been smeared all over my mirror, the toilet tank top thrown into the bathtub, aspirin, midol and tampons mixed into a pile on the floor right next to Felix's feet. If I had any energy left I'd be mortified. As it was, every bit of energy I had was channeled into not throwing up at the moment.

"I'm calling you an ambulance," Felix said.

"No! I'm fine."

"You have a welt on your head, and you were unconscious."

"But I'm conscious now, see?" I pointed out, doing a feeble smile to illustrate my point. "Besides, I don't have any insurance. You know how much an ambulance will cost?"

He pursed his lips together. "We should at least call the police."

"What's the point?" I asked, slowly moving into the living room. I plopped down on the cushionless sofa. "The TV's still here, the stereo. They didn't take anything."

"What happened?" Felix asked, sitting next to me.

"I'm not really sure." I leaned my head back, closed my eyes, retelling the scenario when I walked in as accurately as I could. When I finished Felix's eyebrows were drawn into that tight line again.

"You didn't see who hit you?" he asked.

I moved to shake my head then thought better of it. "No," I said instead. "It all happened so fast. But I'd bet anything it was the same guy who tried to run me off the road."

Felix froze. "Excuse me?"

Oh yeah. I hadn't told him about that.

"What the hell do you mean, 'tried to run you off the road?'" he asked, voice rising.

"It was nothing. Just a scare tactic."

"Who was trying to scare you?"

"Well, if I knew that, I'd have a pretty good handle on who

trashed my place, wouldn't I?"

Felix sighed. Deeply. "Okay, start at the beginning. When did this road rage occur?"

I quickly filled him in on the entire incident. When I was done, Felix grabbed his cell from his pocket and began typing.

"What are you doing?" I asked.

"Sending Tina a message saying she's on the Barker story."

"What?!" I popped up from the sofa, ignoring the way the room played tilt-a-whirl on me, and lunged forward, batting the device from his hand. It clattered to the floor.

"What the hell, Allie?"

"You are not giving away my story!"

"You're kidding, right? You just got attacked in your own home."

"Which must mean I'm getting close."

He shook his head. "It means you've pissed off some very dangerous person."

"Who is scared I'm on the right track."

"Who is trying to kill you. You're off this."

"And Tina's on? So it's okay for her to tackle dangerous stories, but all Allie is good for is the fluff, is that about right?"

"Do *not* make this about you versus Tina," Felix warned.

"Why not? She makes everything about her versus me."

"Okay, fine," he said throwing his hands up. "You know what? Yes. I do see you and Tina differently."

I should have felt vindicated to hear him say the words out loud, but instead more anger bubbled to the surface. "Why? What's so different, huh?"

"For starters, I've never slept with Tina," he said, shouting in earnest now.

"It was only one night, remember?" I shouted back. "You said yourself that it meant nothing."

"Christ, Quick, you're a trained reporter. I'd expect you to be better at telling when someone is lying."

I opened my mouth to shout back again then shut it with a click as his words sunk in. "Wait. You mean... I mean... what do you mean?"

Suddenly my breath caught in my throat, his answer taking on much more importance than I wanted it to have.

Felix swallowed, the fight suddenly dissipating from his face, his Adam's apple bobbing up and down. "I mean…it was a very nice night."

I nodded. "Go on."

"And one I think about."

"You think about it?"

He nodded slowly.

"How often?"

The corner of his mouth quirked upward. "Now there's my crack interrogator."

"Thank you. But don't change the subject. How often? What do you think when you think about it? I mean, do you mean maybe you'd like to do it again? Or maybe you're interested in more than one night? Or that maybe you're interested in me in general? Or just that—"

"Jesus, Allie, shut up," he said. And then in one swift movement he was across the room, his lips covering mine.

They were warm, insistent, as commanding as he was in his editor's role. Only this time I didn't mind. I didn't mind at all. Suddenly a year and a half disappeared, and we were transported right back in time to The Night. I felt all my better judgment going out the window, any tiny voice inside my head telling me not to do this completely drowned out by the rush of hormones Felix's lips created inside me. A rush that started at the soft play of his mouth over mine, charging through my stomach like an army of dragonflies, and ending somewhere south of the panty line in a sensation so warm and urgent it refused to be ignored.

Not that I had any intention of ignoring it.

And from the way Felix's hands had gone around my waist, pulling my body flush with his, neither did he.

He danced me backward toward my bedroom door. We bumped into the end table, knocking my last remaining piece of furniture to the floor, but I barely noticed, my attention focused on getting into that room before one of us exploded. By the time we finally made it Felix's shirt was on the floor, and my tank dress was somewhere near my waist.

I pulled my door open and, as Felix made short work of his khaki's, I grabbed Mr. Fluffykins from his usual spot at the end of my bed and tossed him into the living room amidst howls of protest.

I made a mental note to buy two cans of tuna tomorrow as I shut the door behind us.

Chapter Thirteen

I had to stop doing this. Sleeping with my boss was a bad thing. A very bad thing.

I mean, not that it had been bad. It hadn't. It had been nice. Oh-so very nice, all night long.

I looked over at Felix's face in the glow of the pink numbers from my Hello Kitty clock. It was just before dawn but he was out cold, snoring softly in the dark.

Felix snored.

I don't know why, but that bit of information made me smile. Maybe because I suddenly felt like I was in on some inside joke shared just between the two of us.

I rolled over, turning toward his sleeping form. His features were soft, giving me a rare glimpse of what he might look like if he wasn't yelling at me. His cheeks were dusted with just the finest hint of stubble, giving him a tough, manly air. His lips, a soft contrast, parted gently. It was tempting to lean over and ever so lightly kiss them.

But I was afraid to wake him up.

I wasn't sure what was going to happen when we both faced each other in the light of day again, but none of the scenarios currently running through my head were ones I was dying to play out. Maybe he'd been serious last night when he said he thought about me, that maybe he even had feelings for me. Or maybe he'd just been caught up in the moment. The one thing I knew for sure was that Felix was my boss. We'd been down this fling road before, and it had dead-ended. Only this time, my job was on the line.

So instead of leaning over and sampling Felix's lips like every hormone in my body urged me to, I silently slipped out from under the sheets and pulled a T-shirt over my head. I stepped into a pair of pink fuzzy slippers and shuffled out to the kitchen, hoping the vandals had left my coffee pot intact.

I tiptoed over the mess of broken dishes, finally locating Mr. Coffee. His carafe had been smashed to smithereens against my linoleum, but I pulled a cooking pot from the sink and, after taping Mr. Coffee's sensor down, it worked fine to catch the coffee. I found the only two cups left whole—a chipped "Journalists do it on the front page" mug and one souvenir glass from the Santa Cruz Boardwalk—and sent the machine percolating, the heavenly scent of coffee filling the room.

Between the sprinklers, Gary banging on my door and Felix last night, I think I'd slept a total of seven hours in the last three days. I wondered how long a person could live on caffeine alone.

Not, mind you, that I was complaining at all about the lack of sleep I'd gotten last night. Last night had been an evening well spent. In fact I would gladly live on caffeine for the rest of my life if I could spend every night like that. I felt a goofy grin snake across my face as I watched my pot fill with coffee.

I was still doing the goofy smile when the doorbell rang out a sad little tune. Apparently my attacker had hit that on the way out too.

I quickly crossed the room and opened the door.

And my smile disappeared instantly.

Standing on my doorstep for the second morning in a row was Gary. Today he was dressed in a loud Hawaiian shirt, chinos shorts (that came almost to his ankles) and a pair of red Velcro sandals.

"Morning, sunshine!" he said, pushing his way into my living room. Then he froze, taking in the state. "Whoa. Wild party last night?"

"Hardly," I said, automatically feeling the side of my head. Yep, a big lump was still there. I moved my hair to cover it.

"What happened?"

"Someone ransacked my place," I said, stating the obvious.

"Dude, you really know how to make friends, don't you?"

"What are you doing here, Gary?" I asked, the headache I'd felt from last night slowly returning.

"I came to apologize," he said.

I raised an eyebrow. "Go on."

"For last night. I didn't mean to jump your date. I honestly thought he was attacking you. I mean, when you hired me as a bodyguard I kinda figured you might be in danger, ya' know?"

"If you'll recall, I hired you to be my *assistant*. Not bodyguard."

But he ignored me. "Anyway, I'm sorry I ruined your make-out session with that guy."

"What guy?"

Gary and I whipped our heads around as one to find Felix, fully dressed, standing in the doorway to my bedroom.

Uh-oh.

"Whoa!" Gary said, his gaze pinging from Felix's bed head to my lack of pants. "Dude, you don't mess around. That was a quick bounce back."

"What guy?" Felix asked again, completely ignoring Gary. "Uh..."

"Guess your love life didn't suffer for my interruption last night after all, huh?" Gary said, giving me a nudged and a wink.

Was it wrong to want to hit a guy that much smaller than me?

"Last night?" Felix asked, taking a step into the room. "When you were out with Alec Davies?"

"Um..."

"You were making out with Alec Davies."

I shook my head. "No." I paused. "Well, I mean, I was going to, but Gary stopped me."

"Oh, well, thank God for Gary then, eh?"

"Was that sarcasm?"

Felix shot me a look, then grabbed his shoes and headed for the door.

"Wait, Felix—"

But he didn't let me finish. "Don't be late for work," he spat out. Eyes straight ahead. Jaw set in a grim line. Shoulders tight with a restrained emotion I could only guess at.

Before I could think of anything clever to say he stalked out the front door, slamming it shut behind him so hard that the one remaining picture on my wall fell to the carpet with a thump.

Gary looked from me to the closed door. "Oh. Sorry. I guess I shouldn't have mentioned that whole other guy, right? Yeah, probably not the best idea. My bad."

I could have strangled him. But honestly I didn't have the energy this morning. Instead, I shuffled into the kitchen and poured us both a cup of coffee.

The truth was, it wasn't entirely Gary's fault that Felix left. In all honesty, last night had been destined to end badly from the moment it started. As nice as it had been (over and over and over again...), there were a million reasons why Felix and I were destined to bump into each other for one-nighters only. If it hadn't been Gary sending Felix running this morning, it would have been something else. Frankly, I guess I should thank him for getting it over with nice and quickly instead of drawing it out into hours, maybe even days, of awkward expectations fated from the start to turn into disappointments.

"So, um, what did happen here last night?" Gary asked, sipping from his Boardwalk glass.

I sat down on my cushionless sofa and filled him in on everything, from freaking about Mr. Fluffykins to Felix finding me unconscious on the floor.(though I left out some of the more personal details of my evening, much to Gary's disappointment)

"Dude, rough night," he said when I'd finished.

"No kidding. But at least we know it rules out Alec as a suspect. I mean, he couldn't very well be trashing my place if he was with me at the same time."

Gary nodded. "I suppose. Unless," he said, holding up his index finger. "Unless he hired someone to trash the place and asked you out as the perfect alibi. I mean, how many people knew you wouldn't be home last night?"

I bit my lip, mulling that over. "Actually, anyone could have known. Some paparazzo snapped my photo going into Mangia last night then tweeted about me being there. Anyone could have read it."

"You call the police?" Gary asked.

I shook my head. "No. I convinced Felix not to. The last thing I want is the publicity. If some other reporter gets hold of this story, there goes my angle."

He nodded. "So that means any evidence of the intruder is still here."

I looked around the room. It was one step way from being a junk yard.

"Um...what sort of evidence?"

"I don't know, epithelial cells, hair with DNA tags, fibers, distinct dirt compounds, fingerprints."

I raised an eyebrow his way.

"What? Don't you watch *CSI*?"

"Okay, so assuming some of that stuff is here. How do we collect it?"

He shrugged. "Same way they do on TV, I guess."

While we were clearly no CSIs, I was fresh out of better ideas. So while I showered and changed, I let Gary collect a makeshift evidence kit. By the time I'd thrown on a pair of jeans, a yellow tank top and a pair of white flip-flops with little yellow daisies on them (Yellow was such a happy color. If I dressed the part, surely things would look up for me, right?). Gary had his kit laid out on the remains of my coffee table. I looked down at a container of loose foundation powder, a large make-up brush, scotch tape, tweezers, index cards and a whole crapload of Ziploc bags.

"Is that my Mac foundation?"

"For dusting for fingerprints."

"Do you know how much that costs?"

Gary waved me off, instead taking the top off the container and dipping my makeup brush inside. "Let's start with the front door."

And he did, slowly twirling the brush a couple of inches away from the surface of the front door. Pretty soon my foundation covered every square inch of the doorframe. If there were fingerprints, they were lost in a sea of make-up.

"Hmm," Gary said, looking down at his handiwork. "I think maybe I need a darker color. Got anything else?"

I rolled my eyes. "Maybe we should look for other evidence."

Undaunted, Gary went into the bathroom in search of a darker shade and put me to work collecting hair fibers.

An hour later we had twenty Ziploc bags full of different pieces of lint and hair. I had a bad feeling most were mine.

"I don't think we're very good CSIs," I told him.

"Hang on. I think I've almost got a fingerprint." Gary, tongue protruding out the side of his mouth, was still hunched over my front door, which was now wearing "raspberry glaze" blush, "copper sunset" toner and "midnight mist" eyeshadow. He carefully applied a piece of Scotch tape then lifted it, scrutinizing the surface. "Nothing." Gary blew out a puff of frustration, causing a cloud of foundation to lift into the air. "Surely this guy must have left something behind," he mumbled.

I glanced around. "All right, let's reconstruct the crime." I went to the front door. "First," I said, "he picks the lock, opens the door." I surveyed my apartment from the front door, trying to see the place as if I were a vandal bent on scaring me off the story. "First thing he does is go for the kitchen," I decided. "Maximum impact there, tons to break." I walked into the kitchen, imagining the killer tossing my cupboards. I tried to swallow down emotion at the thought of him destroying my meager but well-loved belongings, instead channeling the stoic Langston and Willows. "Then he'd move into the living room." I did, surveying the damage there, my eyes moving methodically to every spot the vandal must have touched. I paused when I got to the carpet. On it were the remains of several vases, picture frames and porcelain knick-knacks. All smashed. Only, the vandal must have smashed them with something, because my brown renter's shag, while matted down with years of use, was hardly solid enough to break items against.

I quickly scanned the room. It wasn't like I had baseball bats or tire irons sitting around. In fact, there wasn't much of anything that could be used as a weapon, every item of my décor carefully selected for maximum pink and fluffiness. Pillows, throws, the overflow from my closet stacked up in the shelving beside the fireplace. My eyes rested on my shoe tree, toppled over on its side.

"That's it!"

Gary jumped, dusting his hand with foundation.

"The shoe tree. He must have used it to smash the vases and photo frames and stuff. It's the only thing heavy enough."

"Which means his prints would be on it," Gary said, shifting to the item in question, makeup brush drawn. "I'm on it!"

He sprang into action, dipping the brush into the last of my midnight mist and carefully sprinkling the powder onto the trunk of the shoe tree. His forehead wrinkled in concentration, the tip of his tongue making an appearance again while he twirled the brush ever so slowly over the smooth surface. Had it been real wood we might have been out of luck. As it was, my limited budget meant I'd had to go with "wood-like" veneered MDF.

Smooth, slick and perfect for capturing prints.

"I think I got something," he finally said.

I peered over his shoulder.

Sure enough, on the trunk, there was what looked like a fingerprint highlighted by eyeshadow. Or at last half of a fingerprint.

"Hand me the tape," Gary instructed, not taking his eyes off the print as if it might disappear any second.

I did. Then, careful not to disturb the eye shadow, he applied it to the tree. He pushed it down hard, picking up the impression then quickly laid the tape down on an index card.

He stepped back to survey his handiwork. I had to admit, the print had lifted almost as clear as the *CSI* ones did.

The only problem was, we had nothing to compare it to.

"So, what do we do with it now?" I asked.

"We need someone to run it for us." He turned to me. "You got access to any fingerprint databases?"

I bit my lip. Me? No. Felix could access just about any database he chose, but I had a feeling that where I was concerned, he would choose not to. "Not really," I hedged. "Possibly, I could ask Felix, but let's call that Plan Z. What about you?" I asked instead. "You know anyone in law enforcement?"

He bit the inside of his cheek. "One of the contestants on *Little Love* worked as a legal aid to this defense lawyer in The Valley. Tandy. I guess she might have access to some sort of database like that, right?"

I shrugged. It was worth a try.

Gary slipped the index card into a Ziploc baggie then shoved it, along with our millions of fibers, into a paper bag. Then Gary gave me a ride back to my Bug, and we headed toward North Hollywood.

* * *

While Hollywood is usually associated with terms like glamour and celebrity, North Hollywood is Hollywood's dirty little secret. North Hollywood's claim to fame was that it housed more porn studios per square mile than any other place on earth.

We drove past squat concrete houses with chain link fences, dollar stores with bars on the windows and a guy selling knock off Fendi's from his trunk in an alley beside a used car lot full of Impalas and Camaros.

The address Gary got from his little love was situated just off Vanowen between a liquor store and a warehouse with the words "Big Jugs Productions" emblazoned on the side.

I prayed the studio was sound proof as I parked the car, beeped the alarm and followed Gary up a flight of wooden stairs to the second floor of the mustard-yellow building housing "Goldman and Goldstein: we get you off!"

We pushed through the glass front door, entering a generic reception room that carried out the mustard-yellow color scheme with a vengeance. A couple of upholstered chairs and a garage-sale quality coffee table holding a selection of magazines sat up against one wall, a large, oak reception desk taking up the opposite one.

A woman with frizzy brown hair and glasses sat behind the desk, a phone (old-school style, with a cord attached and everything!) glued to one ear. She wore a white button-down blouse, opened low enough that I could tell she had a thing for leopard print undergarments.

Next to her a rotating fan was set to high, blasting lukewarm air throughout the office and rustling a stack of papers on her desk beneath an L.A. Dodgers bobble being used as a paperweight.

"Look, Lenny, we've already gotten your bail posted three times this month... Well, we're running out of bondsmen who don't know your name... I know you got child support payments to make, but if you'd just stop gettin' yourself arrested... All right, all right, I'll see what I can do. Sit tight," she said. Then hung up and mumbled, "Like he's goin' anywhere."

Gary cleared his throat, signaling our presence.

"May I help you?" the receptionist asked, glancing up with a bored expression.

"Hey, gorgeous!" Gary said.

She gave him a blank look.

"It's me. Gary! From *Little Love*!"

She squinted at him behind her glasses. "Ohmigod, Gary!"

She jumped out from behind the desk, and I noticed that she, like Gary, was a little person. She was about a head taller than he was, enveloping him in a hello hug that was all boob. "How are you, doll?" she asked.

"Hmph," came his muffled reply.

"What was that?" She stepped back.

"Doing great now," he told her cleavage.

"Uh, hi," I said, stepping past Gary. "I'm Allie Quick. I'm with the *L.A. Informer*." I offered the woman my hand.

"The tabloid, right?"

I nodded. "Unfortunately," I mumbled.

"Cool. I loved your article on Pippi Mississippi's new hair color the other day. Made me think of maybe going a shade more strawberry myself, ya know? I hear redheads are the new blondes."

"Right," I mumbled, glad I was doing the world a service. "So, um, Tandy—"

"Sarah," she corrected me. "My real name is Sarah Hansen."

"So Tandy was a fake name too?"

She nodded. "The producer of the show said it sounded more fun than Sarah." She shrugged. "Whatevs."

"Listen, we were wondering if maybe we could ask a favor of you?"

"Shoot." Sarah, a.k.a. Tandy, gestured to the pair of upholstered chairs.

I sat down, watching Gary do the same. The fan turned toward us and blew my hair back like a wind tunnel.

"Sorry," she said. "Our AC is on the fritz. It's hell on my hair, ya' know?" she said, patting her frizz.

"No prob." I pulled my own hair back into a knot at the nape of my neck. Which promptly fell out again as soon as the fan rotated. "Anyway," I said, pushing strands out of my face. "We were wondering if you have access to fingerprinting information?"

She pursed her lips. "What kind of information?"

"We have a print, and we need to know who it belongs to. Do you have access to any of those sort of databases?"

She nodded. "Well, not here. But I got a friend at the

precinct downtown who runs stuff for us sometimes."

"Any chance your friend could run this one for us?"

She grinned. "For Romeo here? Anything." She gave Gary a wink.

He winked back.

I had a feeling they were both mentally reliving the hot tub date on the third episode of *Little Love*.

I cleared my throat. "Great. Thanks so much." I pulled our index card out of my bag and handed it across the desk to Sarah.

She turned it over in her hands a couple times. "What's this dust here? Is this eyeshadow?"

I nodded. "Midnight Mist."

She nodded. "Nice shade."

"Thanks."

"Yeah, okay. I'll get this to our guy today. Can't promise he'll be able to get a hit off it. It doesn't look like a full print, but I'll see what I can do for ya'."

We thanked her and left, Gary lingering behind a moment to whisper something in her ear that made her giggle and nod before he hopped into my Bug.

"What was that about?" I asked, as we pulled back onto Vanowen toward the 101.

"What?"

"The whispering and giggling."

Gary grinned. "I got me a date Saturday night."

I raised an eyebrow his way. "I thought you kicked Tandy off on the fourth episode."

He shrugged. "Maybe I acted too hastily. You get a look at that leopard-print bra? Hot."

I rolled my eyes. However, Gary's impending date reminded me of *my* date last night with Alec, and the fact that in the face of my apartment being broken into and the colossally stupid decision to sleep with my boss, I still hadn't had a chance to watch the footage Alec had handed me.

Once we'd cleared No Ho for the trendier Studio City, I pulled into the nearest Starbucks and booted up my laptop. While Gary ordered us a couple lattes and maple scones I plugged in the stick Alec had given me. A couple minutes later the footage started playing.

It was raw, unedited, so it mostly contained a lot of boring stuff like the kids brushing their teeth, Nanny McGregor ushering them all down to the practice room to walk back and forth with adorable smiles for the Barbie doll judges. I hit fast forward, watching the Davenport family zip through their day from various angles. Finally the time stamp on the footage indicated we'd hit the crucial zone when Barker had been murdered.

Gary watched over my shoulder as I let the video play, mentally taking note of who was there and who wasn't.

Nanny McGregor sat in the living room, watching a movie. One of the older girls popped up and asked her for a glass of water. Nanny tucked her back into bed then went back to her movie. About fifteen minutes later, the front door opened and Don walked in. He said hello to Nanny then disappeared toward the kitchen. A couple minutes later a camera caught up to him there, recording mind-numbingly boring footage of him making himself a sandwich—bologna and American cheese—and loudly chewing it. He poured a beer into a glass, drank it, stared out the window a bit. Then he shuffled into the den, flipped on the TV and ordered a pay-per-view movie with a lot of skin and very little plot.

I looked at the timestamp. Twelve-thirty. He'd been home the whole time. No way could he have killed Barker.

I shut the video down, leaning back in my chair with an audible sigh.

"Well, I guess Don's not our man," Gary said, voicing my thoughts.

"No. But you know who we didn't see on that tape?"

"Who?"

"Deb."

Gary shook his head. "No way. I refuse to believe Deb would do anything to harm Barker."

I raised an eyebrow his way. "I take it you're a fan?"

"Have you seen her on the show? She's a frickin' saint."

"Gary, you of all people should know the power of Barker's editing."

"Plus, she's hot."

I rolled my eyes. "She's a mother of twelve."

He blinked at me. "So? She's a total MILF. You know, Mother I'd like to—"

"I get the point," I said, holding up a hand to halt that train of thought before it went into total squickville. "Is there any woman on earth you don't think is hot?"

Gary paused, scrunched up his brow, thinking hard about that one.

"Never mind," I said, "But despite her hotness, Deb doesn't have an alibi."

"She was on her book tour when Barker was killed," Gary countered.

I nodded. "Possibly. But it's also possible she could have flown in for the night, offed Barker, then flown back to wherever her current book stop was, with no one being the wiser."

"Why would she do that?" Gary asked.

I shrugged. "I don't know. Maybe she was tired of being in the spotlight. Maybe she didn't like where Barker was taking her career. Maybe he threatened to expose the truth about the affair to boost ratings next season?"

"That's a lot of maybe's."

"Then I suggest we find out for sure. Let's talk to Deb."

Chapter Fourteen

According to Deb's official book launch website, her tour was scheduled to end today with a mega signing at the Barnes & Noble at the Grove. From 2-4 pm. It was almost one, so we pulled into a drive through In-N-Out Burger and grabbed a couple of double doubles before the signing. Or, I should say, I grabbed *a* double double, and Gary grabbed a *couple* of double doubles. I shook my head at him as he devoured the first one in almost a single bite.

"What?"

"Where do you put it all?" I asked him.

"I told you, I got a high metabolism. Besides, I don't wanna see Deb on an empty stomach. Who knows what stupid shit I might say on an empty stomach."

God forbid.

Half an hour later we were circling the parking structure, looking for a spot within a half mile walk to BN. Which, as it turned out, we needn't have worried about. Because as we exited the structure we saw the line to get into the store spanned all the way around the block, down the next side street, around that block, then doubled back to the first block. There had to be a least a thousand people standing in line to get a signed copy of Deb's book.

I whistled low in my throat. "Wow. I had no idea she was so popular."

"Are you kidding?" Gary piped up. "She only has the most followed Twitter feed in the world."

We took a place in line behind a woman with four little girls in tow and one on the way, if her baby bump was any indication, hunkering down to wait. I looked at my watch. 1:45. I sincerely hoped Deb could sign her name quickly. It would take at least two hours to get through this crowd.

I checked out the other people standing in line and noticed most were, as expected, the mom-looking types—capris, flats, sweater sets or shapeless T-shirts covered in suspicious-looking stains. A few gathered in groups, while some had brought their broods of darlings along with them.

Then, mixed in with Deb's target demographic, were a few guys who looked totally out of place. One wore a suit; another held a bouquet of flowers.

Gary nudged me. "See, I told you Deb's hot. I'm not the only one who thinks so."

"These guys are really here to see her?"

"See her? I'm guessing that guy with the flowers is hoping to do a whole lot more than just see her, if you know what I mean."

I thought back to the pictures of Deb I'd seen. UFO-shaped haircut, khaki shorts, minivan full of rug rats. If that was the kind of woman men went gaga over, I was so misguided.

"Look, we're moving," Gary pointed out as the line inched forward a step. Then came to a halt two paces later.

"How much you think Deb makes on a signing like this?" Gary asked, standing on tiptoes to see through the crowd.

I shrugged. "Beats me."

"Her book's hardcover, right?"

I nodded.

"Okay, let's say it goes for twenty-five bucks. She gets, what, ten percent of that?"

"Probably more like eight."

"Yeah, well, eight makes the math hard, so let's say ten."

I rolled my eyes.

"Okay, ten percent of twenty-five bucks is…" Gary paused, counting on his fingers while his lips moved. "Two-fifty? So, she makes two-fifty per book. There's got to be at least five thousand people here."

"I was going to say a thousand."

"Five thousand times two-fifty…man, she's loaded. I shoulda brought flowers."

"I have to ask," I said, glancing down at the red sandals on Gary's feet.. "What is that on your shoes?"

"What?"

"That outline on the top. Is that Spiderman?"

Gary's eyes shot down to his sandals. "Shit! You can still see him?"

"A little." I paused. "Do I want to know why Spiderman is on your shoes?"

"You know how hard it is to find men's shoes in a size two? I thought I could peel the Spiderman stickers off."

"I'm sure no one will notice."

"Maybe I should just go barefoot when we get to Deb?"

"Look lively, the line's moving again."

Which fortunately, it was. Unfortuntely, it stopped again two feet later.

It took us another half an hour to wind down the first block. Another forty minutes to hit the second. By the time the front door of the Barnes & Noble was finally in sight, it was nearing 4 o'clock, and I was starting to get antsy. Not only because we were nearing the end of the allotted time, but because, thanks to that 32-ounce soda at In-N-Out, I had to pee. Badly. So badly, I felt my eyes glazing over.

"Think we're almost there?" I asked, shifting from foot to foot.

Gary shrugged. "Could be. No idea how long the line is inside the store."

"Inside the store!" I whined. No way was I going to make it.

Four o'clock on the dot, we reached the interior of the place. Unfortunately, that was when the announcement came over the PA system that Deb had to leave, and for the rest of us who had stood in line, she had pre-signed books available for sale.

A collective groan went up from those assembled, the woman with kids in tow in front of us said a decidedly not preschool-friendly word, and people started filtering out the door.

"Great!" Gary threw his hands up. "How are we supposed to interrogate her now?" he yelled.

I wasn't sure. But I knew one thing for certain—if I didn't find a bathroom in the next ten seconds, I was gonna explode.

I frantically peered through the crowd for that telltale faceless blue lady in a triangle-cut skirt. I finally found her hovering over a door near the maps section.

"Wait for me here," I instructed Gary. "I gotta pee."

Then I hightailed to the restroom, shoving through the hordes of would-be book buyers. I think I may have even knocked a couple over. I wasn't sure. All I knew was, nature was calling and I couldn't put off answering any longer.

I pushed through the door, dashed into the nearest vacant stall and let out a big sigh of relief.

I did my business and emerged a new woman. I washed my hands, pulled out some lipgloss, and did a little fluffing of my hair that had fallen woefully flat in the heat outside. I was just about happy with what was looking back at me in the mirror, when a woman emerged from one of the other stalls and made her way to the sink beside me. I checked out her reflection in the mirror.

And almost swallowed my tongue. I'd know that UFO-shaped haircut anywhere.

"Deb Davenport?" I asked.

She looked up. And for a fraction of a second I could see how tired she was before her "on" face slid into place. "That's me!" she cheerfully responded, reaching for a paper towel.

"Wow, I just waited in line two hours to see you."

"Well, I hope it was worth it."

"Sorta. I mean, they told us you had to leave before we even got to the front. But here you are now, so it all worked out."

She did a toothy smile. "Well, it's lovely to meet you. Sorry you had to wait so long. And I'm sorry I don't have any books to sign here," she said, gesturing around herself with a laugh. "They do have several pre-signed at the register, though."

"Actually, I was more interested in talking with you," I said.

Her smile faltered for a half a second. "Really? Well, I'd love to chat about child rearing, but I really do have to go—"

"Actually I wanted to chat about Chester Barker."

The smile didn't so much falter this time as melt from her face faster than a Popsicle on the Venice boardwalk. "Who are you?" she asked. "Who let you in here? Are you media? Because I have nothing to say to you vultures. Nothing!" she reiterated, stabbing a finger at me.

How quickly they turn.

"Listen, I just want to ask you a few questions. It'll only take five minutes of your time."

"I don't have five minutes. I have to be at a photo op at Baby Gap in twenty minutes."

"I'll ride with you!" I offered.

"Ha!" she said. "You really are delusional if you think I'd let you into my car."

She moved around me toward the door. I was losing her. I had to act fast.

"I know you were the one who had the affair!" I blurted out.

Deb froze, hand on the bathroom door handle. Ever so slowly she turned around, her face a perfect void that I'm sure was hard to maintain. "What do you mean?"

"I know that it was you, not your husband, who stepped outside the marriage."

"Who told you that?"

I paused, remembering my off-the-record promise to Don. "A… source."

She narrowed hr eyes at me. "My husband?"

I bit my lip. "Um… kinda?"

"That weak little sonofa—" She remembered who she was talking to and stopped just in time. "Look, my husband will say anything for a little press."

I shrugged. "That may be. But he's way credible enough for me to print an exposé on the *real* reason Don and Deb split up."

"We're back together now, in case you haven't noticed. We had a reunion."

"In Vegas. I know. I also know it was staged."

Deb's complexion lost at least a couple of hours in the tanning booth. "And who told you that?"

"Your husband."

"I'm gonna kill him."

I raised an eyebrow. "Interesting word choice. You feel the same way about Barker?"

"What? No! God, no!" Deb sighed and narrowed her eyes at me again, sizing me up.

"You might as well talk to me," I told her. "Your husband told me everything. If you want your side of the story heard, it's now or never."

She blew a long breath out through her nose. "Okay, fine. You want the real story? I'll give you five minutes. But that's it."

"Sold!"

"Come with me."

I did, following her out of the ladies room. But instead of

going back through the crowded bookstore she turned left, into the employees-only area that funneled off into a warehouse holding dozens of pallets of paperback books. For a second I was overpowered by the scent of new pages, but I had little time to enjoy it as Deb hightailed it toward a door at the rear, where a guy in a dark suit was waiting for her.

"Mrs. Davenport," he said, giving her a nod as he held the door open for her.

She barely registered his existence as she charged through, heading for a limo parked at the curb with the same sort of no-nonsense determination she displayed on the show when charging through her brood of whining tots.

I followed a step behind, half jogging in order to keep up. When she slid into the backseat of the car, I had only a second to do the same before the guy in the suit slammed the door after me and slipped behind the wheel.

As soon as the engine turned over, Deb hit the button to close the barrier between the driver and backseat then turned on me. "Your five minutes starts now."

Nothing like working under pressure. Fortunately, I'd had two hours in line to rehearse what I was going to say to her.

"Tell me about the affair," I said.

She pursed her lips together and, for a moment, I thought maybe she wasn't going to spill it after all. Finally she simply said, "It was stupid."

"Go on."

"Look, you have no idea how much pressure is involved in a show like this. It's not like an actor playing a role who gets to go home and live his life afterward. This is twenty-four seven. Your whole life is on display. Other moms get to have an off day and feed their kids McDonalds. I do it, and suddenly the press says I'm setting a bad example and contributing to the childhood obesity epidemic. I try to discipline my kids, and suddenly I'm abusive. It's like every little thing I do is magnified ten times and broadcast worldwide. It's exhausting."

"And yet you had energy enough for an affair," I pointed out.

"It wasn't like that!" she shot back. She turned to the window, staring at the billboards passing us by on Highland.

"Look, he was understanding. He knew what I was going through. He was a shoulder to lean on. Don and I…every little disagreement we had was blown up on TV. It's no wonder we grew apart, you know? And Barker was always there when things got bad."

I paused. "Wait, Barker?"

"God, it was so easy to be with him."

Mental forehead smack. "*Barker* was the guy you were having an affair with?"

Deb turned to me, surprise evident on her face. "Yes." She paused. "Ohmigod, you didn't know? I just assumed when you said Don told you everything that he'd told you *everything*. Jesus, I thought that's why you were questioning me."

Well, it sure as hell was now. "So, let me get this straight. Barker seduces you—"

"I didn't say that!"

"Okay. He *sleeps* with you. Better?"

She bit her lip, but I didn't wait for a response to continue.

"He sleeps with you. Then when Don finds out, Barker decides in order to save face, Don has to pretend he was the one cheating?"

Deb nodded.

"And Don knew Barker was the other man?" I asked, feeling played that I'd bought Don's don't-ask-don't-tell line.

Deb nodded.

"That gives Don had a hell of a reason to hate Barker. First he bones his wife, then he paints him as the bad guy in the press."

"It wasn't boning!" Deb said, her cheeks tingeing bright red. "We made love. It was…amazing. Special."

I shifted in my seat, suddenly uncomfortable at how my mind flashed back to my own amazing moments last night. Even though I was pretty sure it was not special, a mistake of monumental proportions and had nothing to do with the "L" word.

I cleared my throat, forcing my thoughts to focus on Deb. "How special?"

"I beg your pardon?"

"How long was this affair going on?"

"I don't know," she hedged, picking at a piece of lint on her skirt. "A few weeks. Couple months, maybe."

"Before the nanny walked in on you."

She nodded, still not looking up. "God, how embarrassing. They were supposed to be at practice, but the teacher called in sick or something at the last minute."

"So, the nanny catches you, Don finds out, then what?"

"Then Chester and I broke it off."

"You broke it off, or Chester did?"

Deb consulted the lint again. "What difference does that make?"

Only this—if Deb had considered the affair so special, maybe she hadn't been happy to see it end. Unhappy enough that she might have gone to Barker's house, snapped and gone into if-I-can't-have-you-no-one-can mode, poisoning his wine.

"Where were you the night he was murdered?" I asked her.

Deb's head shot up. "You can't possibly be serious?"

"I only have two minutes left. You think I'd joke with you now?"

She bit her lip. "I did not kill Chester."

"So where were you when he died?"

She put a hand to her head, massaging a space between her eyeballs. "What day did he die?"

I gave her a get-real look. Everyone in Hollywood knew when Barker died.

"Listen, I have twelve children, two book deadlines, a marriage that's crumbling apart and a TV crew at my back. I'm lucky I remember my own name."

"The seventeenth. A Tuesday," I supplied.

"Oh, that's easy then. I have yoga class on Tuesday nights."

"Where?"

"Karma Konnection in Brentwood."

"So I assume someone there can corroborate your story?"

"Of course. The class was packed."

"What time did it end?" I asked, taking mental notes.

Her eyes flickered downward for just a fraction of a second before meeting mine again. "Ten."

I raised an eyebrow her way. "You do know Barker was killed between ten and eleven, right?"

"I...stayed late at class."

"Stayed late?"

"Getting some personal attention from the instructor."

Oh, brother. "You were boning him too?"

"Look, Don and I are in therapy, okay? We're trying to keep things together for the girls. But until he decides he's ready to be a husband one-hundred percent, a woman's got needs!"

"What time did you leave?" I asked, setting the issue of her libido aside for the moment.

"It was well after midnight. Closer to one am, I think."

"And your instructor will verify this?"

She nodded and reached into her purse, pulling out a business card. She flipped it over and wrote on the back before handing it to me.

I looked down. Chad Dharma, and a number with a 310 area code.

"You know, if you're looking for who might have killed Chester," Deb said, "I'd check out that partner of his."

My head shot up at the mention of Alec. "Why?"

"Money." Deb slipped her pen back in her purse. "The company was hemorrhaging money big time."

"How can that be?" I asked. "I mean, he's tops in the ratings everywhere."

"He's also at the bottom. Some of his shows hit, some miss. Lately the misses were outweighing the hits."

That was something Alec had failed to mention. Though, in his defense, I hadn't actually asked, either.

"How do you know this?" I asked.

Deb shot me a look. "I was sleeping with Chester, remember? We talked. Sometimes about work. Chester said Alec was always riding him to cut back. But Chester was a go-big-or-go-home kind of guy. He was all about taking risks. Some of them paid off, but sometimes they didn't. His latest show, *Little Love*?"

I nodded. "I've heard of it."

"Bombed. Apparently little people aren't a novelty anymore, and it turns out the bachelor they chose wasn't all that sympathetic to viewers."

Go figure.

"Anyway, if you want motive, talk to Alec."

I was about to argue that love was just as strong a motive as money when Deb looked down at her watch, then immediately hit the button to open the partition between the driver and us.

"Pull over here," she instructed.

He did, and before I could even ask, he had my door open.

"Your five minutes are up," she informed me.

I looked from her to the driver. "But—"

Deb shot me a look. It was the same one she gave her sextuplets when they whined about wearing itchy dresses on stage. No argument was going to penetrate it.

"Okay," I mumbled. "Thanks for the interview, I guess."

I stepped out, and I swear my feet barely hit the sidewalk before the door shut and her limo peeled off again.

I looked around, trying to get my bearings. I'd been so focused on what Deb was saying I hadn't paid any attention to where we were. Hoping we hadn't traveled to Baby Gap via South Central, I quickly made my way to the nearest intersection and glanced up at the street signs. El Gato and 5th. Wherever that was.

I pulled out my cell and dialed Gary. He picked up on the first ring.

"I've been waiting outside the john for, like, half an hour. Where the hell are you?"

That's what I'd like to know. "I need you to come pick me up."

"Oh great! You mean you ditched me? That's how you do me, huh?"

I rolled my eyes. "I did not ditch you! Deb was leaving. I had to follow her."

"You got to meet Deb!" he whined. "Oh man, what was she like? Was she as hot in person as she was on TV?"

"Just come get me," I told him. Then rattled off the cross streets.

"Where the hell is that?" Gary asked.

"I was hoping you'd know."

* * *

Twenty minutes later I finally spotted my little green Bug with Gary at the wheel. Barely. All I could see was the top of his head over the steering wheel.

He pulled to a stop at the curb, and I quickly switched places with him, scooting him into the passenger seat.

"Thanks," I said, moving the seat back. He had it so far forward I thought I'd fly through the windshield.

"Yeah, well, you can repay me by slipping Deb my number next time you see her."

"Sorry to burst your bubble, but I doubt there's going to be a next time." I quickly filled him in on my interview with the Mom star and her alibi. Then I reluctantly relayed how she'd pointed the finger at Alec.

"But honestly," I said, "I really think she's barking up the wrong tree. Alec doesn't seem strapped for cash."

"Well, we can find out for sure," Gary said. "Let's take a look at the company's financial records."

"Yeah, like he's just gonna hand them to me."

"Well, where does he keep them?"

I shrugged. "They're probably housed at the production offices at the studio. But," I added, "trust me, there is no way we can get on that lot. The only people they let in the gates are movie stars."

Gary nodded. Then he pulled down the passenger side visor and flipped open the little mirror, scrutinizing his reflection. "Huh."

I almost hated to ask... "'Huh,' what?"

"Think I could pass for George Clooney?"

Chapter Fifteen

The plan was simple: get past the gate by posing as movie stars, then sneak into Real Life Productions' offices and get a look at their financials.

Unfortunately, as simple as the plan was, the execution ran into a couple of snags as we pulled up to Sunset Studios. Namely, Gary looked nothing like George Clooney. Or Brad Pitt. Or Johnny Depp.

"Okay, fine!" Gary said after I'd shot down his list of *People's* Sexiest Men Alive. "Who do you think I could pass for?"

I pursed my lips together and took a good, hard look at him. He was short, hairy, and had a face that would give even a mother pause. I was tempted to say he looked like a muppet but that just seemed cruel.

I looked up at the studio lot. The seven-foot-high walls were covered with posters of their top shows and upcoming movies. An action pic starring Stallone, a romantic comedy with Reese Witherspoon and a remake of the remake of the *Little Rascals* starring Elle Fanning and that kid from *Modern Family*.

"Rico Rodriguez," I said, eyeing the poster.

"Who?" Gary asked, his eyebrows hunching together.

"Him." I pointed across the street.

Gary looked up, checked out the *Little Rascals* poster. Looked at me. Then shook his head.

"A kid? Are you fucking nuts?"

"What? You think you can pass as Stallone?" I asked, gesturing to the other poster.

"I got a mustache. Kids don't usually have those," he said, pointing out the facial hair in question.

"Hmm. Yeah. We're gonna have to do something about that."

"Oh, no. No way! We are not *doing* anything."

"You gotta shave it."

"I can't shave! My mustache is my signature. It's my thing! The ladies love the 'stash."

I rolled my eyes. "You can grow a new 'thing', Casanova. Come on, how else are we going to get in there?"

Gary looked from the poster, back to me, back to the poster again. "Jesus, the things a guy does to stay employed."

I did a mental "yes" and pointed my Bug toward the nearest Rite Aid drugstore to grab a pack of disposable razors. While there we added a ball cap and a tootsie pop, and by the time we were done with him, Gary looked at least fifteen years younger. If you looked close it would be obvious that he was a little person, not a child, but I was hoping the security guard's thick bifocals kept him from looking at anything too closely.

I shoved my new ten-year-old in the car and pulled up to the studios gate.

Predictably, the old guy in the guardhouse came out, clipboard in hand. "Name please?" he asked.

"Rico Rodriguez," I answered.

The guard looked in the car.

Gary did a little wave, careful to keep his face shadowed by the cap.

"ID please?" he asked.

I bit my lip. "Um, what kind of ID?'

"Driver's license?"

"He's a kid. He doesn't drive yet," I said, giving the guard a sacchariny sweet smile.

His gaze shifted from my "kid" to me. "And you are?"

"Allie Quick. His nanny."

"Do you have ID?"

"Right here, sir," I said, pulling my own driver's license from my purse.

The guard gave it a once over, comparing the picture to me. While I'll admit I was having a decidedly much worse hair day than the girl in the photo, he finally nodded and handed it back to me.

"Okay, thank you, Miss Quick. I'll buzz you through."

Seriously, I was way too good at this.

Five minutes later we'd stashed my Bug in the lot, grabbed a golf cart—the studio's preferred method of travel—and hightailed it to the fairy-tale looking village of production offices on the left side of the lot. I parked two cottages down from RLP's place, staking out the territory. I knew from my previous visit here that the window to the left of the door looked in on

Barker's office. Predictably, it was empty. The one on the right, however, had a figure pacing in front of it. Since it was Alec's office, it was safe to assume it was Alec.

Also safe to assume his receptionist was sitting in the main room, as he had been when I was there.

"We need a distraction," I mused out loud, getting out of the golf cart. "Something to get both Alec and his receptionist away from the office long enough for us to slip in, nose around, then slip out."

"I got it," Gary said.

And before I could ask what "it" was, Gary grabbed a large rock from the garden of the cottage next door.

"What are you doing with that?" I asked.

"I saw this in a movie once. Totally worked."

He shoved the rock onto the gas pedal and put the cart in gear, jumping clear. The engine revved, the cart's wheels spun and it took off like a shot down the cobbled pathway…

Straight into the last cottage in the row. I watched in horror as it crashed into the porch, taking out the bottom two steps as the railing crashed to the ground.

Immediately doors all down the row popped open, producers and assistants coming out to see what the commotion was.

I grabbed Gary and ducked behind a tree. "What the hell was that?" I whispered.

"You said you needed a distraction."

"Yeah, I said distraction, not destruction!"

"Well, it worked didn't' it?" he asked, pointing to the door of the RLP bungalow where Alec's assistant exited, Alec a close step behind him.

"Come on. We don't have much time," I whispered back, grabbing him by the arm.

We quickly slipped through the office doors then opened the one on our left and ducked inside, shutting it with a click behind us.

The room was laid out the same as Alec's—a large desk in the center, bookcases along one wall holding dozens of DVDs and a couple of file cabinets stacked near the windows. Careful to keep away from said windows, I crossed to the first file cabinet. Of course, as soon as I jiggled the handle I could tell it was locked.

"You see a key anywhere?" I asked.

Gary moved to the desk and opened the top drawer. "Whoa. This guy was a slob."

I peered over his shoulder. Candy wrappers mixed with paper clips, mixed with business cards, loose change and fast food ketchup packets.

"On the up side, no one will be able to tell we've been here," I pointed out, digging in and shifting the random contents.

Ten minutes later we'd gone through all of the drawers, and I was starting to get antsy. I wasn't sure how much longer our wrecked golf cart could keep the receptionist at bay.

I looked under a table, behind a trash can, inside a potted plant. No file cabinet key.

I looked up. As in Alec's office, the walls were covered in huge posters of shows Barker had worked on. Most were stuck up with thumbtacks, but one in the corner was framed and mounted behind glass. The poster advertising the first season of *Stayin' Alive*, the show that had made Barker.

I walked over to it. I lifted one corner and ran my finger along the back side.

Bingo.

I felt the raised metal ridges of a key taped to the back of the poster. I quickly peeled it off, ran to the file cabinet and fit it inside. A perfect match. The cabinet clicked open, and I immediately began pawing through folders for anything that looked like financial records.

"Uh, Allie?" Gary hailed me.

"Yeah?"

"We're out of time."

I whipped my head up to find Gary staring out the window. He was right. The receptionist was on his way back to the office.

No bueno.

I pawed faster, sifting through headshots, expense accounts, show treatments. Finally I hit one labeled "accounts payable." I grabbed it, along with its brother, "accounts receivable," and shoved them into my purse. I stood up and closed the cabinet.

Just as the door to Barker's office flew open.

"What the hell are you doing in here?" The receptionist put his hands on his bony hips, his eyes flashing fire behind a pair of wire-rimmed glasses as his gaze pinged from Gary to me.

"Oh, uh, hi. We...um...I was looking for Alec."

He narrowed his eyes at me. "Alec's office is over there," he said, pointing across the bungalow to the other door.

"Right. Well, see, I um...I was looking for Alec. But then I saw no one was here and I went looking for a piece of paper to write him a note."

His eyes narrowed further. I wasn't totally sure he was buying it, but I did my best dumb blonde hair flip to sweeten the deal.

"Alec had to step out," he said. "But I'll tell him you were here."

"Great. Wonderful. Thanks!" I said, hoping he wouldn't tell him exactly *where* I was here.

I grabbed Gary by the arm and quickly steered him out of the office and down the street before Alec got back.

"Man, that was close," Gary mumbled as soon as we were outside.

"Way too close."

I looked around. But of course, our cart was crashed, which meant we had to hoof it on foot back to the front gate. Which meant that by the time we reached my Bug again I was sweating like a *Biggest Loser* contestant. We pulled out of the Sunset lot and stopped at a 7-11 for slurpies, and I made Gary look the other way while I slipped my bikini bottoms on and my pants off. I'm pretty sure I caught him peeking through his fingers once, but it was still preferable to roasting like a stuck pig in the heat.

We parked under a shady tree a few blocks down from the convenience store and pulled out our boosted files.

Problem was, neither of us were accountants. I squinted down at the printouts. Like most companies, their financial transactions were all calculated online. However, like most executives, Barker must not have completely trusted his hard drive not to eat them, printing out paper copies of every invoice, receipt, and expense filtered through the company. As far as I could tell, RLP was putting out at least three-hundred grand a month in payroll and other expenses.

"What kind of income were they pulling?" I asked Gary, the AR spread open in his lap.

"Hard to tell," he answered, slurping his drink. "Payment comes in chunks, so it's not a regular monthly thing. But as best I can figure, it looks like they were doing fine. Pulling in around two-hundred K a month."

I shook my head. "That's not so fine when you're spending three."

"No way."

"Way." I showed him my file.

"So the company is losing cash," Gary said. "I guess that puts your pretty boy as suspect numero uno again, huh?"

"He's not *mine*. And he's not a pretty boy," I shot back. Though I had to admit it did paint a little more suspicion into Alec's corner. But it didn't exactly scream "smoking gun." A fact I pointed out to Gary. "You know, if Barker was getting desperate for cash, he might have made some desperate programming decisions."

"Such as?"

"Such as revealing Deb's affair after all. I mean, he needed a big season opener, right? What if it came to light that America's homemaker had been cheating all along?"

"What about her books? Her career?"

I shrugged. "Maybe Barker wasn't worried about longevity of the show anymore. Maybe he was worried about a big bang and a big payoff, now. Or," I said, wheels turning in earnest, "what if he planned on cutting some of the big salaries in his other shows? We know Lowel was on the chopping block, but what if he was getting chopped sooner rather than later? Or maybe Barker was getting rid of the other big name judges too? I'd say this spells more motive all around."

"Swell," Gary said, closing the file and using the folder to fan himself. "What do you say you take me back to my air-conditioned car now? It's five o'clock. I need a beer and a shower, and not necessarily in that order."

* * *

I dropped Gary off at his car. Then, as much as a shower and a beer sounded tempting, I pointed my car toward the *Informer*'s offices. I was doing a bang-up job of avoiding fallout from my Disaster Night, even if I did say so myself, but the fact remained that I had a column to turn in.

So I reluctantly parked in the *Informer* lot, threw my pants back on and, holding my head up high, rode the elevator up to the offices. The second the door slid open, my eyes shot to Felix's office.

He was sitting at his desk, Bluetooth in one ear. As if feeling my eyes on him, he looked up, locked eyes with me for a brief second. Then spun in his chair so his back was facing me.

He didn't want to see me any more than I did him.

An odd sensation washed over me. Ninety percent relief, ten percent disappointment. One hundred percent uncomfortable in a way I was way too tired to examine at the moment.

I quickly walked to my cube, turned my back to him, and transferred the notes and raw footage of Don from my laptop to PC, then typed up an article on my interview with Deb, Don's alibi, and the fact that a "reliable source" had informed me RL Productions might not have been the cash cow everyone thought.

I sat back and reread my copy. It wasn't my best work, I knew. It was scattered. Unfocused. Without any clear conclusions about anything. Tons of suspects, tons of scandalous fodder for the tabloid, but no clear murderer. No hard facts. No impressive investigative journalism to make the *L.A. Times* break down my door with employment offer in hand.

I sighed, hit send and shut down my monitor. I glanced at my desk clock: 5:45. If I left now I might be get out of here before Felix read my crap copy. I quickly grabbed my purse and stood up to make for the elevator.

Only I froze as I turned toward the silver doors.

Because someone was getting off. Blond hair, long legs, short skirt, killer high heels. She crossed the office with a confidence few women ever grew into, making me simultaneously hate and want to be her.

I watched as she strutted straight toward Felix's office. She gave a quick knock on the door but didn't wait for a response before entering. Felix looked up, and I watched his face break into a huge, genuine smile. I swallowed, forcing down some lump of emotion I was not in the mood to identity as I watched him jump up from his chair, cross the room, and envelop the woman in a full-body hug.

The way he greeted her, she could have just been a good friend. Maybe a family member. An old schoolmate from years past.

But I knew she wasn't just any of those things.

She was Maddie Springer. And Felix was in love with her.

Chapter Sixteen

Remember that woman Felix was gaga over back when I first met him? The one who ran off and married someone else, leaving Felix so dejected that he rebounded with yours truly?

Maddie Springer.

I stood lamely in my cube, purse in hand, watching through the glass as Maddie laughed, smiled, said something so incredibly funny that Felix burst out laughing too.

I looked at the elevator doors. I could easily slip out now. Felix was totally preoccupied. He wouldn't even notice.

But instead, I sat back down at my chair.

Felix had placed my cube right near his office, ostensibly because with me being the new girl, he wanted easy access to lend a helping hand as I learned the ropes. It was also within perfect earshot of his office.

I turned my computer screen on, pulled up my email program and pretended to read as I focused on the noises coming from Felix's office behind me.

"—so good to see you!" Maddie said. God, even her voice was perfect. Soft and feminine, but still strong and confident.

Felix replied with a, "It's been too long since—"

I strained, trying to make out what it had been too long since for Felix's taste, but a passing car on the street below blocked it out. When I caught up with the conversation again, it was Maddie who was speaking.

"—so glad to get your call. It was out of the blue, but I've been meaning to get in touch. I—"

Dammit, why did cars have to keep driving by!?

"—me too." Felix agreed to something. "Glad you're free this evening. I've been dying to try Mangia, and as luck would have it they happened to have a cancellation tonight."

I bit my lip. He was taking Maddie Springer to Mangia. I had a vision of them laughing, talking, having easy, intimate conversation over a chilled bucket of champagne.

"I can't wait to tell you my news, but let's chat on the way. I don't want them to give our table away," Maddie said.

I heard footsteps behind me and feigned inordinate interest

in my screen as I felt the two of them walk out of his office and toward the elevator. I snuck a peek out of the corner of my vision at the pair. Felix had one arm around her, steering her toward the elevators. Maddie had her right hand on his shoulder, leaning in to whisper something in his ear, her left dangling loosely at her side.

I felt my breath hitch in my throat as I looked at that left hand.

No wedding band.

What did you want to bet the "news" she was giving Felix was that she was newly single and out for a good time?

One I'm sure Felix would enjoy.

I clenched my teeth together, telling myself I didn't care. It was none of my business what Felix did, or who he did it with. Last night had been a mistake. I'd found myself in a vulnerable moment, again, and I'd turned to him for comfort. Again.

But that was it. That was all it was. One night of comfort. I mean, that was clearly all it had been to Felix, or else he wouldn't have gone home and immediately called up his old flame, right? Clearly I was nothing more than a stopover on the way to someone he really cared about. Which was fine. This relationship was purely professional from here on out. And God and the *L.A. Times* willing, not even that for much longer.

I was still pounding that mantra into my head, watching the two of them wait for the elevator, when my cell rang from my purse.

"What!"

"Uh, hi. Allie?" Alec Davies.

I closed my eyes, did a Zen breath. "Sorry. It's been a long day."

"No problem. I'm acquainted with the type. Listen, my assistant said you stopped by earlier."

My eyes shot open. Shit. "Uh, he did?"

"Yeah. He said you were here looking for me?"

"Uh, yeah. Right. I was." I paused, trying to come up with a reason why I might have been looking for him. "I just, um, wanted to thank you again for that footage you gave me. It did confirm Don's alibi," I said.

"Good. I'm glad it was helpful. Listen, I was just about to

knock off for the day. You interested in grabbing dinner with me?" he asked.

"Me? Oh, well, I…" I trailed off. As much as part of me wanted to say yes, the other part was kind of full up on uncomfortable emotions for the day. Alec was hot, funny, smart, charming. Pretty much every girl's dream. Pretty easy to fall for. In all honestly, I'd been a hair's breath from falling right into his arms last night. I blame the champagne, but that fact still remained I was kind of tired of my emotions (and libido) leading my brain around like a stupid puppy.

"Gee, I'm not really sure. I mean, I…"

"You know what? That's okay," Alec said. "I mean, it's last minute, and I shouldn't have assumed you didn't have other plans already."

I glanced up at the elevator. The doors were just opening, allowing Felix and Maddie entry. He gently guided her in with a hand at the small of her back. She turned, flashed him a brilliant smile then leaned in close just as the door slid shut.

"I'd love to!"

"You would?"

"Yes," I said, clearing my throat. "I'd love to have dinner with you tonight," I told Alec.

"Oh. Great! I mean, that's perfect. Tell you what, let me just finish up here and I'll meet you in about an hour?"

"Perfect," I said, then wrote down the restaurant's address before hanging up.

*　*　*

Two hours and one appetizer platter of calamari and cream sauce later, I was definitely not regretting my decision to dine out. Alec had showered, shaved, and smelled like something woodsy and expensive. He was in a black blazer over a white button-down today, the colorless contrast highlighting his brilliant smile and warm eyes. As soon as he'd picked me up, he'd commented on how nice my little black mini-dress was, had called my cat "darling" and then held the door of his Lexus open for me as I climbed in. All the things a guy should do when he's into you. And after the day I'd had, with the guys I'd had it with,

I was really in the mood to appreciate a man who adhered to all the niceties he should.

"So," he asked, leaning across the table of a quaint French bistro on Melrose, "how's your story on Barker coming along?"

"Ugh!" I scoffed, sipping (yes, only sipping this time) from my wine glass. "Don't ask!"

"That good, huh?" He shot me a crooked smile with dimples and everything. "So, I take it you don't have any suspects?"

"Oh, I have suspects in spades. The problem is, everyone seems to have an alibi. Tons of motive, tons of secrets…but unshakable alibis."

Alec grabbed a breadstick and broke it open, buttering half. "Like what? Maybe I can help you shake one down."

I grinned. "That sounded so Humphry Bogart."

"But it made you smile."

"True. Okay, one point for you." I shifted in my chair, taking another sip of the wine, letting it warm my insides as I relaxed into the flirtatious banter. "All right, let's start with Don Davenport. He was caught on tape by your camera crew—thank you again, by the way."

He raised his glass to me. "You're welcome."

"He was caught watching pay-per-view porn, the recorded times giving him an iron-clad alibi."

Alec chuckled. "Not often that getting caught watching porn is a good thing."

"No. It's not. Oh, but his wife has an even better alibi. She was busy doing her yoga instructor."

Alec raised an eyebrow at me. "You're kidding?"

"I wish I was."

"That's priceless."

"Not as priceless as Lowel's alibi."

Alec leaned forward, putting his elbows on the table. "Oh, I can hardly wait."

"He was taking dance lessons. Fandango, to be precise. Turns out, Lowel can't even dance!"

Alec grinned at me. "Well, that one I already knew."

I paused. "Wait, you did?"

He leaned back in his chair and took a bite of his buttered

breadstick. "Of course. Who do you think pays for his dance lessons?"

I cocked my head to the side. "So you knew his whole act on TV was a sham?"

"There's a big difference between a documentary show and reality TV," he said, chewing. "In reality TV you take real people, put them in manipulated situations, edit the hell out of it and, if you're lucky, you get a story at the end. If you're *really* lucky, a story that contains enough drama to keep the voyeuristic viewing public tuning in. 'Reality' doesn't often actually enter into the equation."

I took another sip of wine, digesting this information. "So the other shows—they're all manipulated too?'

He shrugged. "To a greater or lesser extent."

"What about Don and Deb?" I asked, watching his expression closely.

"What about them?" he shot back, his features impassive.

Too impassive.

I felt a sinking weight in my stomach as the truth hit me just how much Alec had been hiding from me. "You knew Don's affair was a floater story, didn't you?"

He paused, took a sip from his wineglass, swished the liquid around in his mouth and swallowed before finally answering. "Yes. I did."

"You lied to me!"

"Look, I didn't *lie*, Allie. You just didn't ask the right questions."

"You knew Barker was sleeping with Deb?" I pressed.

"Yes."

"And you knew the whole reunion was a fake?"

Again he nodded.

"God, is anything real in your world?"

"Allie, this is the *entertainment* industry. In the end it's all about the story, right?" He leaned back in his seat, popped another piece of buttered bread in his mouth and winked at me.

I opened my mouth to respond, but the sharp comment died on my tongue. How many times had I said the same thing? Only now, being on the other end of the philosophy, it sounded almost dirty.

I took a sip from my glass. And I'll admit, it was a big one this time.

"Great vintage, huh?" Alec commented, mistaking my silence for agreement.

I nodded stiffly. "It's great," I said, though in truth I'd hardly tasted it at all.

"I brought it in myself from my own collection. I never trust the local shiraz. Not to be a snob or anything, but California is Cabernet country. The French are the only true masters of the shiraz."

"Hmm." I nodded, sipped more wine, tried to mentally get back to moment five minutes ago when my date was a charming and worldly and not making me suddenly question my own integrity.

"Of course," he went on, oblivious to my internal struggle, "every vintage is unique. Every year a unique combination of flavors. Even from bottle to bottle, things vary."

"You know a lot about wine," I commented.

He grinned, showing off his dimples at me. "I'm a bit of a collector. Though I'll admit, I tend to hold onto bottles longer than I should."

"Don't they just get better with age?"

He shrugged. "Up to a point. But every vintage has its peak time to drink. Past that, it starts to disintegrate into vinegar."

"When's the peak time?"

"Every wine is different. But generally about five to ten years. Barker actually got me started collecting with a great two-thousand four merlot that's just at its perfect peak this month."

I froze, wineglass halfway to my lips, feeling a mental light bulb go on.

"That's it!" I said.

In hindsight, maybe a little too loudly. The couple at the next table glanced our way, the woman giving me a dirty look.

But I didn't care. I had finally hit on it.

"What's it?" Alec asked, confusion furrowing his brows.

"The merlot. The one that poisoned Barker. That's how everyone has an alibi. The poisoner wasn't actually there when Barker died. They didn't poison his glass of wine, they poisoned the *whole bottle*. If Barker thought the vintage was peaking, he'd drink it right away, right?"

Alec nodded. "Definitely. Delayed gratification was not his thing."

"So, someone poisons a bottle of merlot they know Barker can't resist drinking now, then gives it to him as a gift. He takes it home, drinks it and the killer has a perfect alibi of being somewhere else at the time of his death."

"So, who gave Barker the bottle?"

"That's what I need to find out," I said, popping up from my seat.

"Now?" Alec asked, eyebrows drawn together. "But the entrees are on their way."

"Sorry," I said. I looked down at his adorable dimples, his perfect smile, his chic clothes and polished style. "But I have to go. Because, in the end, it's all about the story. You understand, right?" I said, giving him my sweetest smile.

And then I hightailed it out of there as fast as I could, pulling my cell from my purse at the same time.

While the details like the label and vintage of the merlot hadn't been released to the public, I knew for a fact they'd be included in crime scene report. And I knew just one person who had access to the LAPD's database and could retrieve such a report. As much as I really wished I didn't ever have to face him again, I knew that was a pipe dream. And at least now I could face him with a hot lead.

I dialed Felix's cell number from memory, listening to it ring on the other end once, twice. Five rings in it when to voicemail, and I started to worry he was hitting the ignore button. I dialed again as I pushed out onto Melrose, the cool night air hitting my bare arms in a frigid rush. Voicemail again. I immediately redialed as I jog-walked to my car.

Three more tries later, Felix finally picked up.

"What?!" he yelled.

"The merlot!" I shouted back.

"Allie, I don't know what this is about, but I'm at dinner right now and—"

"The merlot that killed Barker was given to him earlier in the day," I quickly cut him off. "That's how he was poisoned, and that's why all our suspects have an alibi. If we can track down where the bottle came from, we can find out who killed him."

There was a pause. And I wasn't entirely sure he hadn't hung up on me. I was just about to ask if he was still there when his voice came through the other end: "Meet me at my house in twenty minutes."

Chapter Seventeen

While it doesn't get much more urban than Los Angeles, the Hollywood Hills is a natural oasis in the center of smog city. Tucked into the southeastern side of the Santa Monica Mountains, they provide stunning views of the L.A. basin, sometimes reaching as far as the ocean on a clear day. Here trees replaced graffiti, the sounds of birds replaced honking horns and the real estate prices climbed higher the farther you drove toward the summit.

Felix lived at the top.

I'd only been to his place a couple of times in the past, but the architecture one could purchase for seven figures never ceased to amaze me. The front of his home was a modern mix of warm, natural woods and sleek, shiny metals. Straight modern lines were accented in slate and stone, butting up against a lush green lawn that spanned around the sides of the house. But it was the back of the house that was absolutely stunning. The entire length of the home was glass walls, all looking out over the valley in a view that took my breath away every time. It was almost as if you were living outdoors, but with the added bonus of year-round air conditioning.

I parked in the circular drive then made my way up the slate walkway to the front door and rang the bell. No one answered. The front windows were dark. I'd beaten Felix here.

I wrapped my arms around myself, shifting from foot to foot in the dark on his front step. It was cold. I thought I heard a coyote bay in the distance, an eerie sound that put me on edge.

I'd been trying my hardest to put thoughts of my trashed place, the welt on the side of my head, and the Escalade driver who tried to run me off the road out of my head. And most of the time I was doing a pretty bang up job of it. But here in the dark, isolated, alone…fear of the boogey man was getting the better of me.

I grabbed my cell and sent Felix a text.

u almost home?

I waited an agonizing two minutes before my cell buzzed to life with a response.

accident on Highland. stuck in traffic. 15 min.
Not soon enough.

I trekked back to my car, opened the glove box, and pulled out my emergency lock-picking kit. There had been a few lessons Felix insisted I learn when I'd joined the *Informer* staff, and Lock Picking 101 had been at the top of his list. I'd honestly been a bit reluctant at first (I had a hard time picturing Diane Sawyer picking locks), but I'll admit it had proven a very useful tool to have in my arsenal on more than one occasion.

Such as when I was stranded outside alone in the dark with a killer on the loose.

I zipped open my little black bag and selected a pick with a long, slightly curved shaped that looked like a dentist's instrument. Then I grabbed a tension wrench in an L-shape. I carefully finessed the pick into the keyhole and felt around. Keyholes are essentially a series of pins that need to have just the right amount of pressure put on each in order to turn the lock. I moved the pick slowly over each pin, testing it with my tension wrench. Most of them moved up and down easily, though one was a little stickier. I focused on that pin first, applying more pressure until I pushed the pin high enough into the cylinder that I heard a click. I slowly let up some of the tension on the wrench and moved on to the next pin, repeating the process.

The first time I'd done this it had taken me half an hour to get all of the pins set. Totally long enough for a curious neighbor to spot me, call the police, and have them cart the tabloid reporter away. I'd done a lot of practicing since then, and I heard the last pin click into place and checked my watch. Two minutes flat. Damn, I was good. I slowly turned the tension wrench and held my breath, hoping I had all the pins set correctly. The knob turned easily in my hand, and the door opened with a silent whoosh of air.

The student becomes the master.

I quickly slipped my wrench and pick back into their case and shoved the whole thing into my pink purse as I stepped inside, shutting the door behind me.

I paused inside the foyer, listening for any sort of alarm system. Nothing. Just the steady hum of computers in the office to my right. I turned on a light, heading toward the sound.

Just off the foyer sat what would have been the family room, though Felix had outfitted it with several computer monitors, scanners, printers and other electronic devices I could only guess the functions of. I took a spot behind the largest monitor, sinking into a well-worn leather chair and jiggling the mouse to life.

The screen asked for a password. I bit my lip, looking down at his keyboard. Unlike Tina's, no telltale signs of wear stared back at me. I tried typing in "informer". No luck. I gave "paper", "story", and "deadline" a try with the same results. I was moving on to adding numbers into the mix when a voice piped up behind me.

"How did you get in my house?"

I spun around in the chair, the sudden break in the silence making my heart leap into my throat.

Felix stood in the doorway, head cocked to the side, a frown marring his features.

"Jesus, you scared me," I told him, sucking in deep breaths.

"You didn't answer my question." His voice was flat, clipped. Completely void of emotion.

I bit my lip.

I'd had about fifteen mental Morning After conversations in my head since this morning about how it was a mistake, how we were caught up in the moment, how we were adults that should be able to put it behind us and work together anyway. Unfortunately, none of those conversations in my head had gone well and with the dark, unreadable look he was giving me now, I doubted real life would play out better. So, I went with Plan B— total denial. Pretend nothing had happened. We were colleagues. Nothing more.

"How did you get in my house?" Felix repeated, taking a step into the room.

"Lock picking set," I answered truthfully.

He blinked at me. "The one I gave you?"

I nodded.

"Remind me not to give you any more presents," he mumbled.

With the terms we were currently on, I didn't think that was going to be an issue.

Holding on to that denial with all I had, I got up from Felix's chair and cleared my throat, trying to clear some of the awkward from the room. "Uh, I was going to log in, but I didn't know your password."

"At least there's one thing you don't know how to break into," he said, taking my place behind the monitor and quickly pounding out his secret word. My instinct was to look over his shoulder, but considering the precarious slant to our relationship at the moment I decided against it, instead watching the monitor as he logged in.

"You said you needed to see the crime scene report?" Felix asked, his tone all business. Apparently two could play at this denial game.

Good. Great. That just made things easier on my end, right?

"Yes. Please," I added. "If we can find out what label of wine Barker drank that night, we might be able to trace the bottle to its owner."

Felix nodded, his eyes never leaving the screen as he pulled up the LAPD's internal website. How he had access to it, I had no idea. And honestly it was probably better for my own deniable criminal culpability if I didn't ask. So I watched as he hooked up a black box to his computer then typed in a string of letters. Rows of numbers appeared on the screen, flashing quickly in long columns.

"What's that?" I asked. Okay, criminal culpability only won out over curiosity for so long.

"Passwords generator."

"Cool."

I thought I saw the tiniest hint of a smile at the corner of his lips.

We watched numbers flash across the screen in silence until finally one of the passwords generated seemed to hit pay dirt, and the monitor changed to a welcome screen for the active cases database. Felix typed in a query for Barker's file. Immediately a list of scanned documents appeared.

"There!" I said, stabbing my finger at a report halfway down the page. Felix clicked the link, and a moment later we were staring at the crime scene report, cataloguing every item found in the victim's vicinity. And there were a lot of them.

Half an hour later we'd read details about every piece of lint Barker had collected on his person, every crumb he'd dropped on his carpet, and every drop of wine spilled within a four-foot radius of the body. I was starting to go cross-eyed, and my back hurt from leaning over Felix's shoulder by the time he finally scrolled down to item number seventy-nine collected by the crime scene techs—the wine bottle.

I held my breath, adrenaline coursing through me as I carefully read the entry. It had been, as I already knew, a merlot. The bottle was dark green, found in the kitchen's recycling bin. Wine residue was still present on in the bottom, though the bottle only contained Barker's fingerprints. The label listed it as a 2004 vintage from Fleurie Vineyards in Napa Valley.

Bingo.

"That's it," I said, pointing at the line. "Can we google Fleurie Vineyards?"

"On it," Felix said, his fingers flying as he pulled up another window. A moment later the vineyard's website filled the screen, photos of grapes and lush greenery on a hillside flashing above info on their tasting room, their address, and phone number.

I pulled out my cell, punching in the number.

"What are you doing?" Felix asked.

"Calling them to ask if any of our suspects bought a bottle recently."

"It's after nine. No one will be there."

I paused. He was right. I didn't realize how much time had passed since my aborted dinner with Alec. "Oh." I shoved my phone back into my pocket.

"Besides," Felix said, the corner of his lip turning upward in a smirk. "I have a better way."

I raised an eyebrow as he pulled up another screen, typing in strings of letter and numbers again. In a matter of minutes he had what looked like an accounting ledger up on the screen.

"Do I even want to know?" I asked, squinting at the font.

"The orders log for Fleurie Vineyards."

"Dude, how did you get this?"

Felix grinned. "Be good, and maybe I'll show you."

I punched him in the arm, quickly scanning the register for the names of our suspects. Ten lines down, one name fairly leapt out at me.

Don Davenport.

"That's it! Don killed Barker!"

"Not necessarily," Felix cautioned. "This proves that Don purchased a bottle of the same wine." He paused, reading off the order. "In fact, he purchased several bottles. Four merlot and two chardonnay. And for all we know, they could still be in his house right now."

I pursed my lips together. "Okay, then let's find out if they are."

Felix shot me a look. "Please tell me you're not thinking what I think you're thinking."

"Okay, I won't."

Silence stretched for a good ten seconds before Felix finally broke. "Dammit, Allie, you cannot break into their house!"

"Oh, come on. You know as well as I do that if I ask him, Don will just lie again. This is the only way to know for sure if that bottle is the one that killed Barker."

"No." Felix stood up, shaking his head. "There's no way I'm letting you do that."

"I'll be careful."

"You're breaking into the house of a person who you think killed a man and tried to kill you as well? What about that screams 'careful?'"

I'll admit, he had a point.

"It's a huge house. What are the chances I'd run into anyone?" I countered.

He shook his head again. "No. Absolutely not. I forbid it."

I put my hands on my hips. "You are not in a position to forbid me to do anything."

"As your boss, yes I am. Do you know how much trouble I'd be in with our publisher if one of my reporters got caught breaking into a celebrity's house?"

"Fine. Then I quit."

Felix froze. "Excuse me?"

"You heard me. I quit," I said with a whole lot more bravado than my meager bank account warranted. It was a brave bluff. If he really stopped paying me I'd have to live on Ramen, and even then I only had a couple weeks between me and starvation.

Felix shut his mouth with a click, jaw going tense, eyes flashing a whole string of unsaid words at me. None of them good. "Fine," he finally spat out. "As of now, you are no longer employed at the *Informer*."

I bit my lip. "Seriously?" I asked, that bravado slipping a little.

"Seriously." And by the set of his jaw, I could tell he meant it.

But there wasn't much I could do about it now. I held my head high and shot back a "Fine" of my own.

"Now, if you'll excuse me," Felix said, gesturing to the front door, "I believe our business here is finished."

"Fine," I said again. Yes, I was completely out of smart comments. I walked with my back as ramrod straight as I could to the front door as Felix kicked me out.

"Oh, and just in case you're still thinking of breaking and entering," Felix said as he held the front door open for me. "Don't. Because if I hear even the slightest whisper of information that the perimeter of the Davenport house has been compromised, I will go to the police with this harebrained plan of yours."

I blinked at him. "You're not kidding, are you."

He gave me a hard look. "No," he said then shut the door in my face.

I spun around, stalked to my car, and gave myself a staunch lecture on how I was not going to cry. So what if I was now unemployed? So what if Felix not only just kicked me out of his house but, by the hard look in his eyes, completely out of his life too? So what if any feelings he may have eluded to were obviously a thing of the past now? So what if he was even now putting the LAPD on speed dial to lock me up?

I didn't care at all. At least, that's what I told that stinging behind my eyes as I made my way back to my Bug.

If that's the way he wanted to play this, fine. I was *so* going to crack this case wide open, *so* going to write the best story ever, and I was *so* getting a position at the *Times* and rubbing it in Felix's smug face.

Only I realized, as I held onto my resolve with a two-fisted death grip, that if I was going to break into Don and Deb's and not go to jail courtesy of one British asshole, not getting caught was priority numero uno. What I needed was a look out. Someone to watch my back as I nosed around the wine cellar.

I mentally went through my options for that someone. But the truth was, I only knew one person who possessed both the qualities of deviousness and drive in quantities perfect for this escapade.

Tina.

Chapter Eighteen

I dialed Tina's number as I zipped down Laurel Canyon, listening to it ring on the other end. Seven rings in, it went to voicemail. I redialed, but she still didn't pick up. Clearly I was being screened. I was going to have to do this in person.

I pointed my car toward South Pasadena, making tracks to the retirement village where she lived with her aunt. Half an hour later I pulled up to her place and parked my Bug at the end of the driveway, blocking any means of escape. She could screen, but she couldn't get away. I walked up the short pathway, past a flock of plastic pink flamingoes tended by a couple of fat garden gnomes, and knocked on the front door.

I could hear a TV blaring in the background, and rang the doorbell for good measure.

A beat later the door was thrown back, and I was face to face with Tina.

She blinked, clearly surprised to see me as a frown settled between her eyebrows. "What are you doing here?"

"I need to talk to you."

She narrowed her eyes. "About what?"

"The Barker story."

She shook her head. "No way, blondie. You need info, you find it on your own."

She moved to shut the door, but I was quicker, shoving my purse in the doorjamb.

"Wait! I don't need info, I have it."

Tina paused. "And you want to share it with *me*?"

I nodded.

Her eyes narrowed again. "Why? What's the catch here?"

"The catch is I know who killed Barker, but I need your help to prove it."

She contemplated this, staring me down for just long enough to make me start fidgeting on her doorstep, before she finally stepped back. "No promises," she warned, holding the door open for me.

I stepped into a small condo with a kitchen to the right that smelled like burnt lasagna and a living room to the left where

Jeopardy! was playing at top volume. An older woman with tight white curls sat on the sofa, eyes glued to the screen behind a pair of bifocals.

Beside her sat a guy with dark hair, dark eyes and a clear addiction to the gym that I pegged as Tina's boyfriend, Cal. I'd heard his name thrown around the newsroom a few times, though this was my first in person encounter. "What is Mount Kilimanjaro?" he shouted at the TV.

"No, it's Mount Fuji," the old lady argued. "Mount Kilimanjaro is in India."

"I think it's in Africa," the guy countered.

"I'm sorry," the host said from the TV, "but the answer is Mount Everest."

Both the old lady and the big guy sat back on the cushions with a collective groan.

"Um, we can talk in the kitchen," Tina suggested, leading the way.

I nodded, following her to a pair of stools set up against a breakfast bar.

"So, what kind of help do you need?" she asked, straddling one.

I took a deep breath, hating that I had to ask but knowing Tina couldn't refuse. "I need you to help me break into Don and Deb Davenport's house."

She raised one heavily lined eyebrow at me. "Because…?"

I spilled all about my wine bottle theory and my argument with Felix. When I finished she had one corner of her lip clenched between her teeth, a frown creasing her forehead. "So, let me get this straight…you actually quit the paper?"

I nodded. Reluctantly.

"So that means I'm the only reporter at the *Informer* working on this story now?"

I slowly nodded again.

"So when we get the proof that Don did this, *I* will be writing the headlining column?"

"For the *Informer*," I emphasized. "I'm submitting my story to the *L.A. Times*."

Tina nodded, turning this deal over in her head. "Okay. Tell you what, blondie, you have a deal. I'll help you."

I let out a whoosh of air I hadn't realized I'd been holding. Phase One: complete. On to Phase Two: the actual breaking and entering.

I waited while Tina changed into a pair of tight black jeans, a black hoodie and a pair of black combat boots. Then she kissed both her aunt and Cal on the cheek, saying she was "going out with the girls". The half-truth seemed to suffice as neither looked up from the TV, still shouting answers at the contestants.

Considering I was still wearing the cocktail dress I'd gone to dinner with Alec in, I pointed my Bug toward home for a quick wardrobe change of my own.

"Whoa," Tina said as she stepped into my apartment. "What happened here?"

"Sorry, it's kind of a mess," I said, flipping on a couple lights (just to make sure we were alone this time).

"And it's really...pink," she said, holding one of my daisy pillows up by the corner as if it might jump up and bite her with contagious happiness at any second.

"I like pink."

"Apparently."

"I'll just be a sec, okay?" I called from the bedroom, throwing on a pair of black stretch pants, a tight black T-shirt, black boots and a black leather jacket. Then I quickly twisted my hair up into a ponytail before joining Tina in the living room again.

I was just transferring a few essentials from my purse to my jacket pockets (driver's license, lipgloss, lock picking set) when a knock sounded at my front door.

Tina raised an eyebrow. "Expecting someone?"

I wasn't. But for a fleeting second I had a vision of Felix standing on my doorstep, tail between his legs to apologize and beg me back to the paper.

A very fleeting second, as I looked through the peephole to find the top of Gary's head staring back at me.

"Hey," he said as I opened the door, not waiting for an invitation before pushing in. "I just came by to—" he stopped when he saw Tina. "Whoa. Who's the new chick?"

Tina narrowed her eyes at him. "Who's the little guy?"

Oh, boy.

"This is Tina. She's…helping me."

"Wait, helping you? I thought I was your assistant?"

Tina shot me a questioning look. "You have an assistant?"

"Sorta. Tina, this is Gary."

"I know who he is. He was on *Little Love*," she said. Then added, "What happened to your 'stache?"

Gary shot me a death look. "I told you it was my thing!"

"You'll grow a new thing. Now, if you'll excuse us, we're kind busy here, Gary," I said, pointing to the door.

Unfortuntely, he didn't take the hint. "So, what's with the outfits?" he asked instead, gesturing to our all-black motif.

Knowing I wasn't going to get rid of him until I did, I quickly filled him in on the wine bottle and the plan to prove it was Don that killed Barker with it.

When I was done he looked from me to Tina.

"So, you guys are going all 'bad girl' on his place?"

I bit my lip. "Kinda."

His face broke into a grin just this side of a leer. "Haaaaaaaawt."

I rolled my eyes. "Exactly what are you doing here, Gary?" I asked.

"I came by to give you the results of the fingerprint analysis Tandy did for us."

Tina leaned in. "Fingerprint?"

"Of whoever trashed my place," I explained. "So, who was it?"

Gary shrugged. "The prints weren't in the database. The person doesn't have a record."

"Great," I sighed. "That doesn't help much."

"Oh, it might," Gary continued, a glimmer in his eye. "The prints aren't in the database because they belong to a child."

"Wait, a child did this?" I asked, looking around.

Gary nodded. "Tandy said the print came back as consistent with the size of a seven- to ten-year-old kid."

My mind immediately went to the dozen seemingly innocent little divas living with Don. "That's it, it's got to be Don."

"How sick that he had his kids trash your place," Tina said, wrinkling her nose as she looked around.

Very sick. Which just made me that much more determined to prove he was Barker's killer.

"So when do we hit Barker's place?" Gary asked, rubbing his hands together.

I paused. "We?"

"Come on, no way am I letting you go without me," Gary said. "Dude, I'm totally helpful. I can be a great lookout."

Considering he couldn't see over my steering wheel, I wasn't convinced of that. But at this point, it was clear we weren't getting away without him.

"Fine. Let's go break and enter."

* * *

It was nearing eleven before we were standing in front of the gate to Don and Deb's estate in Beverly Hills. All the windows were dark, the dozen darlings having been put to bed long ago. I'd parked my Bug around the corner, the three of us hoofing it in so as not to attract attention (well, as little attention as a dwarf, a girl with purple hair and I could attract). We paused, crouching in the bushes to the right of the main gate.

"Okay, boss, how do we get in?" Gary asked.

I glanced up at the huge iron fence running the perimeter of the property. A security camera sat every ten feet, sweeping the area for signs of intruders. Or overly curious tabloid reporters.

"There," I said, spying a section of fence a few feet to our left. A large oak tree stood just inside the gate, its branches hanging low over the fence. Providing just enough cover from any security cameras. "That's where we go up and over."

"Awesome," Tina said, breaking into a grin that showed off a mouthful of white teeth in the dark. If I didn't know better, I'd say she was enjoying this.

"Whoa," Gary said. "You mean climb over the fence?"

"You have a better idea?" I asked.

Gary looked up at the fence. He looked down. "Fine. But I'm gonna need a boost."

The three of us scuttled to the oak tree. Then Tina and I acted as one, lifting Gary—who was surprisingly heavy for someone so short—until his hands grasped onto the top of the fence, and he hauled himself over. He paused a moment at the top then fell forward, tumbling down the other side. I cringed as he belly-flopped into a bougainvillea plant on the other side.

"You okay?" I whispered.

"Peachy," came his muffled sarcastic reply.

"I'm coming over," I answered, quickly hoisting myself up, landing thankfully on my feet on the other side. Tina hopped over in a second, making me wonder if this was her first breaking and entering attempt.

The three of us (with Gary still wearing a couple of flowers stuck in his hair) ran up the expanse of lawn between the fence and the main house, thankful for our dark clothes to keep us in shadow. Instead of going to the front, we took a chance and circled around the back of the house, hoping for a less conspicuous point of entry.

We found one just behind the kitchen window: a back door leading into what looked like a laundry room. Predictably it was locked tight, but the lock was a far less sophisticated one than they'd employ in the front of the house. I quickly pulled my kit from my pocket, selected a pick and went to work.

"You carry a set of lock picks?" Tina asked.

I nodded. "Don't you?"

"I will now," she answered, and I couldn't help feeling just a little pleased at the note of respect in her voice.

"How long will this take?" Gary whined, looking over my shoulder.

"Shh. I'm almost there."

Which was true. Three short minutes later I felt a tell-tale click and the knob turned in my hand.

But before I could step through, Tina rushed past me into the house. "We have sixty seconds," she said, charging through the laundry room.

"Until?" I asked, as Gary and I jogged after her.

She shot me a look over her shoulder. "Before the alarm system goes off and wakes the entire house."

Right. Alarm system. I hadn't thought of that.

But apparently Tina had, as she made a beeline through the laundry room, down the hall and straight toward the front foyer. A white panel hung just inside the doorway, and she quickly flipped it open, punching a series of numbers into a keypad. A moment later a green light flashed, giving us the all clear.

"Okay, I give up. How did you know the code?" I asked.

Tina grinned. "I watched the raw footage from the night Barker died. Don had to punch in the code when he got home."

I blinked at her. "Wait—how did you get the footage?"

She shrugged. "I hacked your computer after you left today."

If I wasn't so impressed, I'd have been livid. As it was, I was totally glad Tina was on my team that night.

"Hey girls," Gary said, hailing us from down the hall. "I think I found the wine cellar." He pointed to a doorway under the stairs. Sure enough, as we looked through, a second set of stairs lead downward toward a basement area beneath the house.

I led the way, slowly descending the dark stairway until it opened up into a small room containing a maze of wooden shelves, lined floor to ceiling with wine racks. I looked around, feeling my spirits sink. There must have been hundreds of bottles. It was going to take us forever to look through them all.

Gary took the fork to the right, I took the one on the left, and Tina snaked down the aisle in the center. We worked in silence, each isolated in our own section of the maze, checking the labels of each bottle for so long that my back started to ache from being crouched at the lower shelves. I was just about to concede that Felix was right about the harebrained quality of this plan when I spied a label on a bottle of white wine with the same grapevine logo as the Fleurie Vineyards website.

I quickly grabbed it, reading the label. Bingo. It was the chardonnay Don had purchased. I put it back, checking the next bottle. A Fleurie merlot. I quickly pulled the next few bottles out, counting off two chardonnay and three merlot. There was one bottle missing.

The one that had poisoned Barker.

I moved to go tell Gary and Tina we'd hit pay dirt.

But I never got the chance.

As I spun to my left, I caught only the slightest glimpse of a wine bottle flying toward my head before pain exploded at my temple, my vision blurring, and the polished hardwood floor of the cellar rushed up to meet me.

Chapter Nineteen

A heavy metal drummer had taken up residence in my head. Or at least that's what it felt like when I finally came to. I had no idea how long I was out, but it was long enough for a whopper of headache to gain a foothold between my ears. I lay as still as I could, concentrating on not throwing up as I felt that drummer bang against my temples from the inside. After a few moments it subsided to a dull roar, and I braved opening my eyes. I blinked slowly, trying to get my bearings.

I was on the floor, somewhere cold and hard. It was dark and, if you didn't count the pounding in my own head, silent. As my eyes slowly adjusted to the lack of light, I saw a mirror along one side of the room, my own reflection staring back at me beside a line of wooden props and judgmental dolls. The divas' practice room. Don must have knocked me over the head and dragged me here. I wondered how long ago that might have been. Or, more importantly, how long until he came back to finish me off.

That thought spurred me to try moving, starting with my fingers. They worked, but I didn't get further than a small wiggle because I quickly realized my hands were tied together behind my back with some sort of rope. I looked down, just barely making out the shape of my own feet in the dark. Yep, they were bound too.

Fabulous.

"Allie?" I heard a low whisper from somewhere to my right.

I squinted in the dark. "Gary?"

"Oh, thank God, you're alive!"

"Where's Tina?" I croaked out.

"Here," another voice answered, just beyond Gary.

"What happened?" I asked, wiggling into a sitting position as I blinked through the blackness. I could just make out her form a few feet away.

"I don't know. One minute I'm looking at cabernets, the next I'm on the floor."

"Ditto," Gary said, and I could hear him rubbing the back of his head. "Where are we?"

"The Davenport's basement," I answered. "Don must have

dragged us all down here."

"Or Deb," Tina said.

I turned to her. "Deb?"

"Yeah, you know, I've been thinking. Why not Deb? She had access to the bottle, access to the kids to trash your place."

"No way," Gary chimed in. "Hot chicks don't kill people."

Tina shot me look. "Where did you find this guy?"

"Hey. I'm right here!"

"Do you really think Deb is strong enough to carry all three of us down here?" I asked, ignoring Gary.

Tina shrugged. "Why not? I'm not that heavy. What are you, a size ten?"

"*Six*," I shot back under my breath.

Tina's snort said she didn't totally believe that, but she let it go. "So, neither of us is that big, and Gary's kid-sized—"

"Hey! I'm short, not deaf. I can hear you, you know!"

"—so it's totally possible she could drag us down here one by one."

"Possible, I guess. But my money's still on Don," I countered. "He had way more motive to want Barker dead than Deb. Besides, he lied to me about not knowing who his wife was sleeping with."

"News flash, New Girl: lots of people lie to tabloid reporters. That doesn't mean they're killers."

I bit my lip. "You know, I really hate it when you call me New Girl."

"Oh yeah? Well, you know what I really hate?" Tina asked, inching closer to me. "Being knocked over the head and tied up!"

"Don't tell me you're trying to blame me for this?" I shot back, scooting toward her.

"Um…duh! This whole thing was your idea."

"Well, at least I *had* an idea. At least I had a lead to follow."

"I have plenty of leads of my own!" Tina shouted back, getting right up in my face now.

"Yeah, ones you stole from my computer."

"Oh, you're one to talk! I know you were looking at my coroner's report."

"Dude," Gary piped up. "Cat fight. Hot."

"Shut up," we both yelled at him in unison.

"Wow, and people say *I* have anger issues."

"Gary, I swear to God…" I started.

"Quiet, someone's coming," Tina interrupted me.

I shut my mouth with a click. She was right. I heard footsteps on the stairs above us. I bit my lip, listening in the dark, feeling Tina and Gary do the same as Don…or Deb…came closer.

At any other time, three on one odds were pretty good. But when all three were tied up, I didn't like our chances of making it out of this estate alive.

A door at one end of the room opened, and light suddenly flooded the room. I blinked against it, feeling my pupils contract painfully as I squinted to see which Davenport was shadowed in the doorway.

It wasn't until the door shut again and the overhead lights turned on in the practice room that I saw which one of us had been correct about the killer's identity.

And was shocked to realize we were both wrong.

"What a terrible nuisance you all have caused," Nanny Nellie Mc Gregor said, her lilting voice taking on a sinister tone as she held a gun straight-armed in front of her.

"Dude. The hot nanny!" Gary said. "Totally didn't see that one coming."

I'll admit, neither had I.

"Wait, you killed Barker?" Tina asked. And I was glad to hear my own surprise mirrored in her voice.

Nanny nodded slowly. "Yes. Yes, I did."

"But why?" I asked.

She cocked her head at me. "He was evil. What he was doing to the family, to the children, it had to be stopped."

"What was he doing to the family?" Tina asked. I felt her twisting her body toward Nellie, her hands coming up against mine. Or, more specifically, the ropes holding her hands together. Instinctively I backed up, my fingers exploring the knots at her wrists. If just one of us could get free, we might have a fighting chance.

"The children's lives were being torn apart by that beastly show," Nellie went on. "Cameras everywhere, paparazzi stalking them," she said, spitting out the word as she sent an accusatory look Tina's way.

Tina shrugged. "Sorry?"

"Sorry is right! Sorry is what their lives had become. A sorry excuse for a childhood."

I felt my fingers slip beneath the first knot, slowly loosening it as Tina shifted closer.

"So what did you do?" Tina asked, clearly trying to keep Nellie talking, trying to buy us some time.

"I did the only thing I could do! Deb and Don didn't care about the girls. All they cared about was the money and the fame. What their poor excuse for parenting had bought them. Their children became a distant second to their careers." Nellie snorted. "As if they'd even have careers without those poor girls."

"Hey, Deb has a lot on her plate right now," Gary piped up, defending her.

Nellie spun the gun his way.

Gary squealed.

"So you had to protect them," I asked, getting us back on the path of distraction. I could feel the first knot slip loose. A couple more minutes, and Tina would be free.

"Yes," she answered, an eerie calm coming over her voice as she turned back to me. "I had to protect them. I'm all they have. I did the best I could to shield them from the craziness, but when I saw Deb in bed with Barker, I knew he had to be stopped. And there was only one way."

"So you killed him," Tina said.

Nellie nodded. "It was easy, really. All I had to do was inject some of Deb's anti-depressants through the wine cork. I told Barker it was a gift from Deb."

"And once he was dead, the filming stopped," I noted.

She nodded, her face breaking into a smile. "Everything has been so nice. The children have been so happy these last few days. So normal."

"Except for you taking them to trash my place. That's hardly normal kid stuff," I pointed out.

She frowned, my accusation of being a bad influence on the kids clearly digging deeper than that of being a murderer. "I told them it was a game. They had a wonderful time smashing your dishes."

I'll bet.

"Then smashing me over the head?" I asked.

"Certainly not!" She shook her head emphatically back and forth. "I had them wait in the car for that."

"Well, aren't you a model caregiver," I couldn't help saying.

"I am! I take care of those girls and anything else that needs taken care of around here!"

"Like us?" Gary squeaked out.

"Yes. Like you. Like you nosey, no-good tabloid reporters digging where you have no business being."

"Technically, I'm no longer on the *Informer*'s staff," I pointed out.

"Shut up!" she shouted. And since she punctuated it by shoving the gun in my face, I did.

"So now you're going to kill us too?" Tina asked. I could feel her hands slipping from the knots, wiggling free. "Kill us right here in the girls' rehearsal room?"

Again, the frown settled between Nellie's eyebrows, as if appalled that we'd even think such a horrible thing of her. "Of course not."

"Oh, thank God," Gary sighed.

"I'm going to take you into the closet and kill you there. I don't want to wake the girls."

I think I heard Gary squeal again

"And," Nellie went on, looking right at me, "I'm going to start with you."

My heart leapt into my throat as she pointed the gun at my head and took a step toward me.

Then everything happened at once. Nellie's hand clamped around my arm, I felt Tina's hands slip free, and then Tina jumped up from the floor like a jack-in-the-box, hurtling herself straight into Nellie.

Surprise registered on the nanny's face for a split second before she toppled backwards, the gun going off in her hand as she fell, taking out a Barbie and a chunk of the mirror with her.

Gary screamed, crawling into a fetal position.

I dove for the weapon but considering I was still bound, couldn't do much with it. I twisted onto my back, trying to fit my fingers around the trigger as I watched Tina wrestle on the ground with Nellie. Tina had the element of surprise on her side, but Nellie had the advantage of having both her hands and feet free. One she used to the fullest, wrapping one leg around Tina's middle and pinning her down.

"Grab the gun!" Tina yelled, pulling at Nellie's hair.

"I'm trying!" I shot back. I had my fingers around the pistol, but with my hands behind me I couldn't very well see where I was aiming. I twisted, contorting my body until I thought I had Nellie in my sights, and pulled the trigger.

A shot rang out, accompanied by a piercing scream. It took me a second to realize it was not Nellie's.

"Oh my God, you shot me!" Gary yelled.

Oops.

"Sorry! Gary, are you okay?" I asked, twisting to face him. A thin trickle of blood oozed down his right arm. If I had to guess, it was a minor flesh wound. But Gary took one look at it, saw the blood, then his eyes rolled up into his head and he promptly fainted.

Great. Some bodyguard he was.

"A little help here!" Tina shouted. She was still grappling on the floor with Nellie, and if I had to guess I'd say Nellie was winning. Tina had a chunk of Nellie's hair still twisted in her fingers, but Nellie had her hands around Tina's neck. And Tina's face was quickly turning the same shade of purple as her hair.

Chucking the gun, I inch-wormed across the floor toward them, bringing my legs up to my chest and shoving my bound feet toward the nanny as hard as I could. She grunted, falling to the side, her grip loosening enough that I heard Tina suck in big gulps of air.

I pulled my feet in close, coming in for another attack again, but Nellie was faster, rolling to the left before I could connect.

Tina moved to grab her leg, but the lack of oxygen slowed her reflexes and before she could even make contact, Nellie was on her feet again.

And reaching for the gun.

"That's enough!" she yelled, all semblance of British

propriety gone as she stood over us, pointing the weapon our way. Her hair stuck up in tufts, missing a small section on the side. Her cheeks were flushed, eyes wide, breath coming in pants. "I've had enough of all you tabloid reporters!"

And before either of us had a chance to react, she squeezed the trigger, popping off two shots.

Right at Tina.

"Uhn." Tina made a gurgling sound in the back of her throat then fell backwards, her head connecting with the hardwood with a dull thud.

"No!" I yelled, immediately inching toward her.

"Don't move!" Nellie shouted.

The barrel of her gun was suddenly in my face.

I held my breath, frozen like the proverbial deer in the deadlights. Time seemed to stand still, my mind racing.

This was it. I was a goner. I'd never be an *L.A. Times* reporter. I'd never have a chance to thank Tina for trying to save my life. I'd never see Felix again.

For some reason, that last thought brought tears to my eyes, blurring my vision as Nellie's finger closed around the trigger. I steeled myself for the sharp sting of a bullet ripping through my body.

But it never came.

Instead, Nellie grunted, her eyes rolled back in her head, and she keeled over forward, slumping into a pile on the floor.

I blinked, my eyes going from her to the guy standing behind her.

All four feet of him.

"Gary," I breathed out on a sob.

He held a wooden lollipop prop in both bound hands like a baseball bat, glaring at the lump he'd just created on the back of Nellie's head.

"Never mess with a little person," he panted, "with anger issues!"

Chapter Twenty

The next few hours were a total blur. Turns out, Nanny McGregor was right about the noise of a gun in the rehearsal room waking everyone up. Don had called the police after the first gunshot, saying there was an intruder in his basement. The authorities arrived only minutes after Gary brained Nellie, bursting into the rehearsal room as both Gary and I frantically did CPR on Tina. Luckily, the responding officer knew CPR a whole lot better than we did (and his hands weren't bound together), so he managed to get a pulse while he radioed for a paramedic.

I could have cried with relief when they finally arrived, taking Tina's prone form away on a stretcher as the number of cops in the Davenport house multiplied several times over. I found myself telling the same story to about fifteen different officers, until finally a guy in plainclothes took pity on me and had a uniformed officer drive me home.

As much as I just wanted to collapse onto my bed and sleep for a hundred years, I forced myself to boot up my laptop first, my fingers typing out the story of my life. When it was done I quickly emailed it off, for the first time in my career completely at peace with where it would be published in the morning.

I had just enough energy left afterward to do a quick call in to the hospital to check on Tina's condition. She was in surgery. I took that as a good sign, noting the visiting hours tomorrow before I crawled into my bed, fully clothed, just as the sun was beginning to peek through my blinds.

* * *

I awoke to the sound of my cell phone ringing instantly from my nightstand.

I rolled over. 8 am. I'd slept a whole two hours. I thought a really bad word as I grabbed my cell and stabbed the on button.

"What?" I croaked.

"May I speak with Allie Quick please?"

I cleared my throat. I swore to God, if this was a

telemarketer…

"This is she."

"Well, good morning, Miss Quick."

"That remains to be seen," I mumbled.

"Excuse me?"

"Never mind. Listen, is this about some subscription or something? Because I'm really not interested right now."

"Oh, I'm sorry. This is Mr. Callahan. From the *L.A. Times*?"

I sat up in bed so quickly I felt my neck seize up on me. "Mr. Callahan. Oh, wow, sorry. I didn't realize. It's…so nice to hear from you."

"I apologize for calling so early, but I wanted to be the first to get to you before the other papers get their bids in."

"Bids?" I asked, my foggy brain trying to process what he was saying. "What bids?"

"For your services."

"I'm sorry. I'm not following…"

"We'd like to offer you a position on staff."

I blinked. "Could you repeat that?"

Mr. Callahan chuckled genially on the other end. "I know, I know, I should have done this weeks ago when you first interviewed with us. I apologize, but honestly you just didn't seem to have the experience then. But with this Barker article I just read, well, clearly you're a reporter who knows how to get to the heart of a story. And has the guts to do it, too. That's something we value here, and we'd love it if you reconsidered joining our team."

"Joining your team as…" I trailed off, remembering the women's column.

"As an investigative reporter. We'd assign you to the local beat, but I assure you you'd have free rein over what sort of stories you investigated."

I must still be asleep. This was a dream, right? "You're serious?" I asked, my voice rising two octaves.

"Absolutely!"

"I…wow…I…I don't know what to say."

"Well, tell you what? Take the morning to think about it then get back to me. How's that sound?"

"It sounds wonderful!" I said.

I hung up floating somewhere about two feet above my body. The *L.A. Times* wanted *me*!

* * *

Since there was no way I was falling back to sleep now, I got up, showered, dressed, added an extra layer of mascara to detract from the dark circles forming under my eyes and drank about a gallon of coffee. Then I hopped into my Bug and headed toward the hospital, stopping only briefly in the gift shop to buy a big purple balloon that said "Get Well Soon" on it before making my way to Tina's room.

The white-haired aunt and the boyfriend were both there too, Cal holding one of Tina's pale hands in his, his forehead pinched in a look of concern that said he'd been in that position most of the night. The top part of Tina's torso was wrapped in a big white bandage, tubes going from her to a machine in the corner that beeped out a steady rhythm. Though I noted her eyes were open, which I took as a positive thing.

She turned my way as I entered the room and managed a feeble smile.

I waved back. "Hey."

"Hey."

I cleared my throat. "How you feeling?" I asked, setting the balloon next to her bed.

"Like shit."

"Figures." I paused, biting my lip. "You gonna be okay?" I asked, hating how my voice cracked a little on the last word.

Cal piped up. "The doctors said she was lucky. Both shots missed any vital organs. The muscles in her shoulder are pretty torn up, but with some physical therapy they expect her to make a full recovery."

I let out a sigh, realizing just how relieved I was to hear that. "That's good. Really good."

"Not being shot would have been better," Tina said, rolling her eyes. "But what can you do?"

"About that," I said, taking a step closer. I took a deep breath. "I, um, wanted to thank you. For saving my life back there. If you hadn't jumped Nellie when you did, she would have shot me for sure."

Tina blinked at me a minute, trying to gauge how sincere I was. Finally she must have come to the conclusion that I wouldn't mess with a woman in her condition, as a small smile curved the corner of her mouth. "Yeah, well, I guess we're even then. If you hadn't kicked her off me, she would have strangled me."

"Occupational hazard, I guess," I joked.

Tina nodded, though I could see her smile waning. As little sleep as I'd gotten, I could tell she'd had even less.

"So, um, truce?" I asked. I held a tentative hand out toward her.

She looked down at it. Up at me. Then the semi-smile made another brief appearance, and she grabbed it. "Truce."

Honestly? I didn't realize until she said it how much that word would mean to me.

I left her to rest with a promise to come back later that afternoon with a stack of magazines, a couple books and some decent take-out. Then I pointed my Bug toward Hollywood, steeling myself for one more uncomfortable conversation.

I parked in the *Informer*'s lot, then forced my feet one in front of the other up the flight of stairs, my bravado wavering as I hit the familiar newsroom. Keyboards clacked and phones rang, the smell of toner and freshly shampooed carpets permeating the air. Cam was in the corner, conversing over an obit picture with Max. And I spied Gary sitting at Tina's desk, staring at her monitor.

But I didn't stop to chat with any of them, knowing that if I didn't do this now, I might never. Instead, I charged right into Felix's glass walled office, not pausing to knock, and locked the door behind me.

Felix was behind his desk, Bluetooth in one ear, fingers hovering over his keyboard. He looked up, surprise clear on his face.

"Listen, I gotta go," he told the person on the other end of his Bluetooth. "Something…just came up."

I waited while he hit the off button, then pulled the device from his ear.

He stared at me.

I stared back.

He cocked his head to the side.

I cleared my throat.

"Hi," I finally said.

He nodded. "Hi."

I cleared my throat again. "I, uh, saw Gary out there…" I trailed off. Which wasn't what I'd come to say, but I was buying time to muster more of that bravado.

Felix nodded. "Tina's going to need some help for a while. I hired him as her assistant."

I couldn't help a grin. Poor Tina.

"So, um, I take it you read my story?" I asked.

He nodded. "It was very good."

I nodded. "I thought so too."

"I was surprised when you emailed it to me. I thought you didn't write for the *Informer* anymore."

"I know. But that story belonged here. Tina and I worked together on it."

"I noticed you put her name on the byline too."

I nodded. "She deserved it."

He nodded back. "I agree." He paused. "So, why are you here, Allie?"

I sucked in a deep breath, swallowing every last ounce of pride I had left. "I'd like my job back," I said.

Felix raised an eyebrow at me as the words hung awkwardly in the air. "Why? I thought you were waiting for a position at the *Times*?"

"I was," I admitted. "They offered me one this morning."

Something flickered behind his eyes. "And?"

"And I'm turning them down."

That something flickered again, stronger this time, as Felix took a step toward me. "Why?" he asked quietly.

I licked my lips. "I…I like working here."

He raised an eyebrow. Took another step closer. "You do?"

I nodded. "Yes. I like digging where no one else dares to dig. I like Cam, and Max, and…I even kinda liked working with Tina," I admitted.

"And?" Felix asked. He'd edged closer again. So close he was just inches from me.

I licked my lips again. "And…I like working with you."

"*Working* with me?"

I nodded.

"That's all?" he asked, his voice so low it was almost a whisper.

I moved to nod again. But he was so close. Sounded so intimate that I couldn't lie. Instead, I shook my head slowly from side to side. "No. That's not all. I like…" I swallowed. "You."

"Me?"

I nodded. "Yes."

"As in…?"

I rolled my eyes. "Seriously, I have to spell it out for you? I'm into you. I dig you. I want you, okay? And not just for one night. Only, I know you're totally into someone else, so I know that night didn't mean anything…and that *other* night didn't mean anything, either. But I'm okay with that. Well, not totally okay, but I can get okay if being not okay means we can't work together anymore, okay?"

Felix blinked at me. He frowned. "What someone else?"

"Maddie. I saw you with her. After the night we… Well, I saw her in your office. It's obvious you're still in love with her. Which, like I said, I can be okay with, I mean I'll get over—"

"I'm not in love with Maddie," he cut me off.

"Oh, please, Felix. You call her up 'out of the blue,'" I said, doing air quotes, "take her out to a romantic restaurant. She's glowing like a teenager and *not*, I might add, wearing a wedding ring anymore. Felix, I'm not stupid. It's obvious you still have feelings for her."

Felix stared at me. Then a slow grin spread across his face.

I bit my lip. "What? What's with the grin?"

The grin turned into a chuckle, then he said, "If that's the kind of investigating you do, I'm not sure I want you on staff at my paper."

I narrowed my eyes at him. "What do you mean?"

"I mean, I called Maddie to ask her to dinner because she'd sent me three emails in the last week saying she had news to tell me. I felt guilty I hadn't had time to return any, so, when I got a reservation to Mangia I figure I would make it up to her."

I opened my mouth to respond, but he didn't let me, instead

continuing.

"And the news, in case you're wondering, is that Maddie's pregnant."

I shut my mouth with a click. "Pregnant."

"Yes. She's not wearing her wedding ring because her fingers have swollen."

I swallowed hard. "So she's not getting a divorce?"

Felix grinned bigger, shook his head. "No. She and her husband are deliriously happy together, and they're expecting a baby boy next year. In the spring. Anything else you'd like to know? Because I have the name of her midwife if you'd like to confirm."

I shook my head, feeling my cheeks turned bright crimson. "No, I'm good."

Felix took a step toward me. "You know," he said, the grin widening even further, "you're adorable when you're all jealous like that."

"I was not jealous!"

Felix raised an eyebrow at me.

"Okay, fine. I was a little jealous. Just," I held up my thumb and index finger, "maybe *this* much."

The grin returned, all teeth.

I cleared my throat. "So…do I get my job back or not?"

Felix gave me a long look. Some of the teasing went out of his eyes for a moment, genuine emotion shining as he scrutinized me. "I'll make you a deal," he finally said.

"A deal?"

He nodded, his lips just inches from mine now. "I'll give you your job back," he said, "if…"

"If?" I breathed.

"If Mr. Fluffykins sleeps in the living room again tonight."

I felt a big goofy smile snake across my face as Felix leaned in, his lips hovering over mine.

Now that was an offer I couldn't refuse.

Chapter Twenty-One

Tina did, I'm happy to report, make a full recovery. The truce, however, lasted all of two days after she got back to the office, suffering a quick death when Felix gave me the story about the break-ins at several prominent Hollywood nightclubs and gave Tina the story about Pippi Mississippi's new boyfriend. She tried to say it was because I was sleeping with Felix, even though it was honestly more due to the fact that Tina's arm was still in a sling and she had to take public transportation everywhere (not that I was denying the sleeping with Felix). But even though our healthy rivalry was alive and well again, I noticed she had stopped calling me New Girl. Which I took as a sign that deep down, a part of our resident Bad Girl really did love me. Just maybe very deep down.

Surprisingly, Gary proved himself to be a useful asset to the *Informer*. It's amazing how many places a "child" can gain access that a tabloid reporter can't. So even after Tina recovered, Felix agreed to keep him on as a junior reporter.

One of Gary's first solo assignments had been to cover the trial of Nellie MacGregor, who ended up taking a plea bargain that would put her behind bars until every one of the diva dozen was out of high school. Both Don and Deb had been appropriately appalled with the thought that they'd hired a killer to watch their children. It had been a sort of wake-up call, and rumor had it they'd both cleared their schedules to spend more time at home with their kids, even canceling their appearances at all the Gold Coast pageants for the summer.

Lowell Simonson had pleaded no contest to stabbing Barker and got off with a hundred hours of community service. Cam had run photos of him just last week fulfilling some of those hours by teaching the tango to seniors at the Pasadena Community Center.

As for Alec, I never talked to him again. He called me a couple of times after I left him in the restaurant, but I honestly didn't know what to say back, so I never returned his messages. But he was handsome, charming, and a top Hollywood producer, so I was pretty sure he was going to do all right in the romance department.

Real Life Productions, on the other hand, did not do all right.

Three months after Barker's death they closed their doors, marking the end of all the shows Barker had created. On the one hand, I was kinda sad to see it go, as *Stayin' Alive* really had become an American staple. On the other, Barker's legacy had already spurred on a whole new generation of reality TV. Just last month Tandy, Mandy and Candy from *Little Love* had all signed on to do a show for FOX where they would compete to win plastic surgery procedures, called *Little People, Big Boobs*. Gary, of course, already had a running list of ways to sneak onto the set.

"Hey, Quick." Felix called me from his office, diverting my attention from the article I was typing up on the latest nightclub break-in.

I popped up from my chair, sticking my head in his office a second later. "Yeah, boss?"

"Where are we on the break-ins?"

"Five in the last month," I said, counting off on my fingers as I approached his desk. "Three-hundred thousand stolen in cash, and hundreds of credit card receipts."

"Any leads?"

I shrugged. "The cops are baffled. No fingerprints, no fibers, nothing left behind."

"Pros," Felix concluded.

I nodded. "Looks that way. Thing is, they must have someone on the inside because they bypass every security system."

Felix raised an eyebrow. "All use the same company?"

I shook my head. "Nope."

"Then it's got to be someone working the clubs. Get a name of all the bouncers that moonlight the area and start working through them, one by one. Get Tina to help."

I nodded. "On it."

"And Allie?" he added as I turned to go.

"Yeah?"

"That was a pretty long lunch you took."

I grinned. "Sorry. I was at the mall."

"The mall?" he asked, raising an eyebrow. "We have a story there?"

I shook my head in the negative. "No. There was a sale."

"A sale?" Felix repeated.

I grinned again. "Uh-huh. At Victoria's Secret."

Felix's other eyebrow headed north. "Really. Purchase anything nice?"

"Be good," I said, giving him a wink, "And maybe I'll show you."

About the Author

Gemma Halliday is the author of the *High Heels Mysteries*, as well as the *Hollywood Headlines Mysteries* series. Gemma's books have received numerous awards, including a Golden Heart, a National Reader's Choice award and three RITA nominations. She currently lives in the San Francisco Bay Area where she is hard at work on several new projects.

To learn more about Gemma, visit her online at www.GemmaHalliday.com